For the first ti home, he kisse
meant it.

At first Olivia stiffened, bracing her hands against Jamison's chest, but then, like sweet ice cream melting in the heat of the sun, she softened and she kissed him back.

So what if he was being territorial? He had good reason. They were good together, and it took something like this to remind him that they belonged together.

His lips found her earlobe, her jaw, her neck, and he trailed possessive kisses down to her collarbone. He knew he had to stop. The driver was waiting and if he didn't stop now, he'd sweep his wife up in his arms, take her upstairs to their bed and prove exactly how much he loved her.

Dear Reader,

Did you ever want something so badly you didn't know how you'd survive without it? How far would you go to get it? Those are the questions plaguing Olivia Armstrong Mallory, daughter of the founder of the Armstrong Fertility Institute.

On the outside, Olivia seems to have it all—she's young, beautiful and married to the man of her dreams, Jamison Mallory, the oldest son of a wealthy political dynasty. He's heralded as a future contender for the U.S. presidency. Olivia plans to be right there by his side when he makes his bid for the White House. The only thing missing from their picture-perfect life is a baby.

As Olivia comes face-to-face with her worst nightmare, she realizes that all the money and power in the world can't buy the things that matter most—love and family. In the process, she discovers a capacity to love that she didn't know she possessed.

I hope you enjoy Olivia and Jamison's journey. I love to hear from readers. So be sure to let me know what you think. You can reach me at nrobardsthompson@yahoo.com.

Until next time,

Nancy Robards Thompson

THE FAMILY
THEY CHOSE

NANCY ROBARDS THOMPSON

SPECIAL EDITION®

Published by Silhouette Books

America's Publisher of Contemporary Romance

Special thanks and acknowledgment to
Nancy Robards Thompson
for her contribution to THE BABY CHASE miniseries.

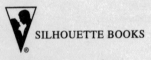

SILHOUETTE BOOKS

Recycling programs
for this product may
not exist in your area.

ISBN-13: 978-0-373-65508-3

THE FAMILY THEY CHOSE

Visit Silhouette Books at www.eHarlequin.com

Printed in U.S.A.

Books by Nancy Robards Thompson

Silhouette Special Edition

Accidental Princess #1931
Accidental Cinderella #2002
*The Family They Chose #2026

Harlequin NEXT

Out with the Old, In with the New
What Happens in Paris (Stays in Paris?)
Sisters
True Confessions of the Stratford Park PTA
Like Mother, Like Daughter (But in a Good Way)
   "Becoming My Mother..."
Beauty Shop Tales
An Angel in Provence

*The Baby Chase

NANCY ROBARDS THOMPSON

Award-winning author Nancy Robards Thompson is a sister, wife and mother who has lived the majority of her life south of the Mason-Dixon line. As the oldest sibling, she reveled in her ability to make her brother laugh at inappropriate moments, and soon learned she could get away with it by proclaiming, "What? I wasn't doing anything." It's no wonder that upon graduating from college with a degree in journalism, she discovered that reporting "just the facts" bored her silly. Since she hung up her press pass to write novels full-time, critics have deemed her books "funny, smart and observant." She loves chocolate, champagne, cats and art (though not necessarily in that order). When she's not writing, she enjoys spending time with her family, reading, hiking and doing yoga.

This book is dedicated to Gail Chasan and Susan Litman. Ladies, thank you for your patience and commitment. Working with you makes me a better writer.

Chapter One

The chime of the house alarm alerted Olivia Armstrong Mallory that someone had opened the front door, rousing her out of her light sleep. The door squeaked open and then clicked shut, the sound echoing in the cavernous hallway.

As footsteps sounded on the parquet floor, she sat up on the couch, smoothed her brown hair and blinked at the Christmas tree—the sole light illuminating the expansive living room.

She'd only closed her eyes for a moment—or so she thought. However, a quick glance at the mantel clock begged to differ. It was after three in the morning.

Jamison.

Her husband had finally arrived home.

As a United States senator who was being groomed for the presidency, Jamison Mallory wielded a lot of power, but one thing beyond his control was the weather. It wasn't his fault that ice and snow had grounded all planes coming in and out of Washington, D.C.

It's a wonder he's home now, she reminded herself as he appeared, suitcase in hand, in the archway that divided the living room and the foyer hall.

"Liv, you're still awake?" His deep voice was flat. "You didn't have to wait up for me." Even in the low light, she could see that his handsome face looked drawn. His chiseled cheeks looked hollow, despite the day's growth of blond razor stubble. The dark circles under his pale blue eyes hinted that he suffered the kind of travel-weary exhaustion that comes from long flight delays and blisteringly cold weather.

"Of course, I waited up for you. It's Christmas Eve, Jamison—well, it was. Merry Christmas." Olivia stood and smoothed the wrinkles from her red silk dress. She made sure the clasp to the pearl necklace she always wore was in the right place. When her husband didn't move toward her, she swallowed her pride and crossed the room to him.

One of them had to extend the olive branch. In the spirit of Christmas, and for the sake of their marriage, she'd be the peacemaker tonight.

Two-and-a-half months apart—with only a brief Thanksgiving Day visit—was more than enough time to help her realize that her marriage was *that* important. In their seven years of matrimony, this trial separation was the longest they'd ever been apart.

She'd missed her husband so much it hurt—a deep, gnawing pain that only grew worse each day they were apart.

Jamison set down his bag and raked a hand through his short, wavy blond hair before opening his arms to her. Olivia slipped inside the circle of her husband's embrace and tried to find that place where she fit so well. She wanted nothing more than to bury her face in his chest, to lose herself in the feel of him. But his hug felt stiff, almost perfunctory. As she shifted to find *her spot,* he dropped his arms and pulled away ever so slightly.

She hesitated a moment, processing the conflicting emotions that swam to the surface as she stood face-to-face with this handsome familiar stranger. But, no, she wasn't going to make an issue of it. So she slammed the door on the irrational thoughts goading her to take his aloofness personally.

Spending Christmas Eve stuck in the airline's Executive Lounge surely wasn't his idea of a good time. He must be so tired and—

"You must be starving." She started toward the kitchen. "I kept dinner warm for you. Sit down and I'll fix you a drink and a plate."

She glanced over her shoulder in time to see his frown deepen as he shook his head.

"Olivia, I'm exhausted. I just want to go to bed."

His brusque tone made her wince. As was often the problem between them, it wasn't so much *what* he said, but *how* he said it that cut her to the quick.

Tonight, though, she was willing to overlook it.

"Yes, of course," she said. "I can see that you're worn-out."

He picked up his suitcase, walked over and kissed her on the forehead. Then, without another word, he turned and took his bag into the first-floor guest room, closing the door behind him.

Olivia stood alone in the living room. Confused, she crossed her arms over her chest, trying to ward off the numbing chill coursing through her. She could understand that Jamison was bone tired. She could even accept that he didn't want to eat a meal and go to bed on a full stomach. But choosing the guest room over *their* bed?

That hurt worse than his gruff tone.

Suddenly, the cold distance between them yawned like a vast canyon, full of all the reasons they'd decided to separate in the first place.

She'd had such high hopes for the evening. But nothing was turning out as she'd hoped.

Wasn't that par for the course these days?

It hadn't always been that way, though. Once upon a time, not so long ago, their love seemed invincible. There was nothing like it from the moment they'd set eyes on each other. She'd never forget the first time she saw him. In person, that is, because every red-blooded woman in America knew of Jamison Mallory, *Panorama Magazine*'s "Sexiest Bachelor in the Universe" for several years running. With his tall, bronzed, quarterback body and his All-American blond, blue-eyed good looks, the man simply needed to flash his lightning-strike smile and women fell under his spell.

As a Harvard Law graduate and the youngest elected U.S. senator, Jamison had come back to his alma mater to deliver a commencement address. They'd bumped into each other—literally—as Olivia rounded a corner, rushing from one of her classes to a rehearsal for a Harvard Ballet Company performance of *Sleeping Beauty.* She'd dropped her dance bag and books and he had helped her retrieve her ballet slippers from underneath a shrub. Somewhere between, "Excuse me," and "It was so nice to meet you, Olivia," he'd asked where she was going and she'd nervously rattled off information about the ballet performance, which was the next night. She had never dreamed he'd be in the audience—front and center.

Because he was *Jamison Mallory.* She was simply a shy, college freshman who'd barely had any experience with men. After all, up until meeting Jamison, her one true love had been dance.

Later, they'd both sworn it had been love at first sight.

He'd often said that from the moment he'd looked into her eyes as he handed her those slippers, he'd known he'd met the woman he would spend the rest of his life with.

"It was cosmic." He used to flash his devastating smile when he'd tell that to reporters. "The feeling was so much bigger than anything I'd ever felt before, I knew it was right."

Now it was the small things that stood between them and what was really important. The minutiae blurred the perspective so that they couldn't keep the big picture in focus anymore. If they couldn't get past the small stuff, how in the world were they going to reach the real issue that was keeping them apart?

Feeling as if she were dragging a heavy weight, she made her way into the kitchen to put away the uneaten dinner. She and Jamison had always spent Christmas Eve with her family and Christmas Day with the large Mallory clan at his mother's palatial compound in the Berkshires. This year, she'd opted out of Christmas Eve with her mother, father and three siblings—all of whom were married to their careers at the Armstrong Fertility Institute. Well, except for her brother Paul who, though he was still the consummate workaholic, had recently met his love match in Ramona Tate, at the institute. Olivia wanted to spend their first night back together alone. Just the two of them. Little had she known how alone she'd actually be.

Staying home had seemed like the right thing to do at the time, especially since none of the family knew about her and Jamison's current living arrangement—that Jamison hadn't come home on weekends during the congressional session. Or that he'd stayed in Washington after the session had adjourned. They'd told everyone he was busy with a particularly demanding committee, that he needed to focus so that he could wrap up work in time for Christmas. They'd played their roles so well that no one had a clue that their marriage was actually deeply in trouble.

Olivia hoped to God she'd find a Christmas miracle in her stocking, because it seemed as if nothing less than a miracle would save them now.

Jamison awoke to a slant of sunlight streaming in through the white plantation shutters, hitting him square in the face. He blinked, disoriented for a moment, and then it all flooded back to him. He was…home.

He glanced at the clock on the bedside table: seven-thirty. Although he could've told the time without the clock, thanks to his internal alarm. No matter how little sleep he'd gotten the night before—in this case only about four hours—his system awakened him at seven-thirty every morning. It was fail-safe, and there was no sense fighting it. He might as well get up, because he wouldn't be able to go back to sleep. Plus, he and Olivia needed to get on the road by noon to make the two-hour trek to his mother's for the Christmas Day festivities.

He stretched, and his arms slid over the cold, empty side of the queen-size feather bed. He wished he was waking up in his own bed, with Olivia in his arms, rather than realizing another morning alone—

especially Christmas morning in the guest room of his very own house.

He'd been so exhausted by the time he'd arrived home last night, he'd barely been able to string together a coherent sentence, much less have a discussion with her about sleeping arrangements. After being separated from Olivia for two-and-a-half months, he wanted to be fair to her. Even though sleeping apart from her wasn't what he wanted, he didn't want to seem presumptuous on their first night back together—and even more, he didn't want to fight.

He'd been beyond exhausted and, yes, a little cranky. He knew himself well enough to know that combination was a recipe for disaster. But now, in the bright light of morning, his head felt clearer, his purpose stronger. Eager to talk to his wife about their next step in their relationship before they joined his family for the annual Christmas Day festivities, he showered, shaved and dressed before making his way toward the kitchen in search of a good, strong cup of coffee…and Olivia.

The house was dark and quiet. Even before he flicked on the kitchen light, he could see that the room was pristine—everything in its place. The only evidence of the dinner Olivia had offered him last night was the ghost-aroma of something delicious mingling with the faint scent of dish soap and the slightly smoky traces of the fire that must have blazed in the fireplace.

He breathed in deeply, relishing the familiar, comforting scents of home. But as he did, guilt tugged at him. He knew his wife had not only prepared a delectable Christmas Eve feast that neither of them was able to enjoy, but she'd probably stayed up long after he went to bed putting everything away and cleaning up the mess of a dinner that never happened.

The least he could do was let her sleep a little while longer and then make her some coffee.

No, he'd go one better and surprise her with breakfast in bed.

Before their separation, the kitchen had been foreign territory to him. One thing he'd learned in the time they'd been apart was how to cook up a mean batch of scrambled eggs—the trick was to use low heat so that they cooked slowly and the outside didn't scorch. Hmm…the low-heat approach would also benefit their marriage. Because the other thing he'd learned during this time apart was that he loved his wife desperately. He missed her…he missed *them*. It was time to put all the ridiculous fighting and blaming behind them and move on.

Time to use the *low-heat* approach.

And to think the root of their problems started over

something that meant so much to both of them, the common ground on which they'd always met: family. Or, more specifically, the lack of a family of their own.

Cold, twisted confusion wrapped around him when he thought about it. He was so torn. On one hand, Olivia would make such a wonderful mother. On the other, how could they even bring children into the world when their marriage was so shaky?

When they weren't even living together?

They had to talk about their relationship. They had to get back on track. But before they could get into that, he had to break another bit of news to her—the news that he had to return to Washington earlier than expected. Earlier as in *tomorrow* morning, rather than January third as they'd planned.

That would go over about as well as telling her that the holidays had been canceled this year. With the way their plans had been preempted, that wasn't so far from the truth.

Jamison made his way toward the stainless steel refrigerator and tugged opened the double doors. The precise arrangement of the cartons, jars and stacked glass and plastic containers echoed the kitchen's tidiness.

One of the many things he admired about his wife was the pride she took in their home. He'd encouraged her to hire a cook and a full-time housekeeper so that she'd have more time for herself and time for the Children's Home, a non-profit orphanage where she sat on the board of directors. But she'd refused, because she loved cooking—and was darn good at it. She's said while it was just the two of them she could get by with someone coming in and doing the deep cleaning a couple of times a month. She claimed she enjoyed keeping their house, making a home for them. When it came to home and family, there was no one more dedicated than Olivia. That's why their fertility issues had been such a struggle. They desperately wanted children and had jumped through many hoops to get pregnant—all to no avail. Too much testing and too many treatments had set them on an emotional roller coaster and taken a serious toll on their marriage. How ironic, when marriage had to be the bedrock on which the family was built.

Liv wouldn't take well to the suggestion, but he'd been thinking about asking her to agree to put having children on hold until they could heal their marriage. It was the only thing that made sense.

But one thing at a time. First, he had to break the news about the change of holiday plans.

Jamison found the eggs, butter and cheddar cheese and was just turning around with his hands full when Olivia walked into the kitchen.

"Good morning," he said. "I thought you'd still be asleep."

She shook her head. "I thought you'd sleep in since you got home so late."

She didn't sound like herself, and she looked at him with a wariness that took him aback. But she did look beautiful standing there perfectly made-up and dressed, wearing the pearls that he'd given her as a wedding present, her dark hair twisted up in a way that accentuated her porcelain skin, fine cheekbones and gorgeous dark eyes—deep brown, like the coffee he craved almost as much as he thirsted for her.

"What are you doing?" Her voice was flat. She sounded tired.

He adjusted the goods in his hands, fidgeting as if he'd been caught trespassing. This was her territory after all. In the seven years they'd been married, he'd barely set foot in the kitchen, much less cooked a meal.

"I thought I'd fix you some breakfast." He grinned sheepishly, suddenly feeling out of his league.

"You don't have to do that." She gestured toward the items in his hands. "Just put those things down and I'll do it. I have a special breakfast planned."

Oh. Of course she would, it being Christmas.

"Well, I just thought—" Their gazes snagged for a brief moment before she looked away. With that, he knew beyond the shadow of a doubt that something was wrong. Of course something was wrong, but he'd been so bent on moving forward with the next steps they should take to fix things between them that he hadn't counted on having to delve backward into their problems before they could move on. Suddenly the clarity he'd felt moments before was replaced by a dread that riveted him to the wooden kitchen floor.

Olivia walked toward him and took the food from his hands. Then she set to work, returning the cheese to the dairy drawer and removing various other items from the refrigerator and pantry. Jamison stood and watched her for a moment, feeling superfluous.

Since she hadn't made any moves to start the coffee, he decided it would be a good task and began opening cabinet doors to locate the beans.

"What are you looking for?" Olivia asked.

"Coffee," he replied.

"It's in the freezer." She gestured to the drawer below the refrigerator. "I keep it there so it will stay fresh since I'm not drinking it these days."

"Really? So, no coffee for you?"

She shook her head.

"How come? You love coffee."

She turned and squinted at him, looking plenty annoyed. "Jamison, I haven't been drinking coffee for the past two years. Don't you remember the doctor suggested that I cut caffeine from my diet while we were trying to get pregnant?"

Well, it was an honest mistake since they hadn't had the opportunity to *try* during the past couple months. Even so, he thought as he rummaged through the freezer drawer, his not knowing felt like a failure. Funny how he felt perfectly at home on the senate floor, where he knew every nook and cranny of the issues he passionately presented, yet he'd forgotten that the doctor had nixed caffeine from his wife's diet.

Bad show, man.

When he pulled out the unopened bag of whole-bean French roast, Olivia was right there ready to pluck it from his hands.

This time, he held on tight.

"I can do it," he said.

"Since when do you know how to make coffee?" she asked, tugging every so slightly, but he refused to let go.

"Since I haven't had you to make it for me," he said, looking her square in the eye. For an instant, a look—surprise, hurt, disappointment…maybe a combination of the three—flashed on her face.

"I'll make it for you," she insisted. Once again her expression was flat and there was no warmth in her eyes where mere seconds ago there had been a pileup of emotion.

The distance between them was killing him. He had to do something.

He glanced down at their hands still holding on to the bag of coffee. They were so close, yet not touching. He stretched his finger until it touched hers. She flinched and snatched her hand away, leaving him holding the bag of French roast.

She looked startled for a moment then turned back toward the kitchen counter, busying herself with the breakfast preparation, taking eggs from the carton with shaky hands.

"Liv," he said. "We need to talk about this. It's not just going to go away."

She placed the eggs in a bowl and stilled but didn't respond.

"I don't know about you," he said, "but I've missed you so badly it's tearing me up."

He saw her grip tighten on the edge of the counter until her knuckles turned white.

"I'm sorry last night didn't work out the way we'd hoped. I wish you would've gone on to your parents when we realized my flight was delayed."

He saw her shoulders rise and fall, and dreaded delivering the news that he had to leave tomorrow.

"It wasn't your fault, Jamison. I know that."

She turned to face him. "But sleeping in the guest room last night—that was your choice."

"What?" As tightly wound as she appeared, he was expecting her to unleash what was bothering her, but he wasn't expecting this to be part of the problem.

"You heard me." She was clutching her hands in front of her, again gripping so tightly that her knuckles were turning white. She looked so small, so fine-boned and fragile standing there, it was a wonder her fingers didn't snap like twigs.

"Liv, I was exhausted." He ran a hand over his face. "I didn't know up from down. I couldn't even form the words to ask you where you wanted me to sleep."

He reached out and touched her hands, hoping the gesture would encourage her to relax. "But it's a new day and there are a few things we need to talk about before we head up to my mother's place."

Olivia's face shuttered, but he saw her throat work as she swallowed.

"Such as?" she asked.

"Such as whether or not we should tell the family we're separated. Despite how much I love you, I can't go on pretending. What are we going to do, Liv? What are we going to tell them?"

Chapter Two

The moment they turned onto Stanhope Manor's long, cobblestone driveway, Olivia could see that the Mallory mansion was bursting at the seams with family and festivity.

Lights, decorations and a blanket of new-fallen snow transformed the stately home into a winter wonderland. An army of children ran and played on the rolling lawn. Some made snow angels; others joined forces in a collaborative snowman building effort. The bittersweet sight of all those children brought tears to Olivia's eyes.

She wanted to believe that someday her kids

would play on that lawn, but she and Jamison seemed further away than ever from having a family of their own. That morning, the double whammy of a Christmas present he'd dropped into her lap was not only that he was returning to Washington early, but also that he wanted to put their baby plans on the back burner. It was the last thing she'd expected. The last thing she wanted. Because of that, the two-hour ride up to the Berkshires was mostly silent. What more was there to say? They were officially at a standoff. Jamison insisted they shouldn't have children until they were happy as a couple; Olivia couldn't see how they'd be happy until they had a baby. Or at least *she* couldn't be happy. Not with Jamison spending more and more time away from her.

They were supposed to spend Christmas week together, but he'd said something about an unexpected diplomatic visit. She'd always prided herself on being supportive of her husband's demanding career. But lately it seemed the more she gave, the more one-sided their life became. And balance didn't seem to be a part of Jamison's New Year's resolutions.

She tried to persuade him that this was the perfect example of how there was no *perfect* time to have children. It was simply another excuse to wait. Even worse, she didn't understand why he felt compelled to wait. She got the distinct feeling that he wasn't telling her the real reason behind his hesitation. But no matter how many times she told him having children was exactly what they needed to mend things, he'd come back around to "We need to fix *us* first."

So, what was she supposed to do?

Passively give in?

Just give up?

No way would she do that. Not when their future depended on it.

So they'd reached a standoff, except for agreeing to not saying anything to the family about their separation until they'd had a chance to talk more. That seemed code for "Let's continue this vicious cycle of pretending." She had a sinking feeling that they were set on a collision course with disaster.

As Jamison steered the car under the porte cochere, anxiousness threatened to pin Olivia to her seat. She really wasn't in a mood to put on a happy face for her mother-in-law and extended family. After the disastrous discussion with Jamison, this masquerade felt beyond her. But the alternative of announcing their marital problems to the bunch was worse. With one last wistful glance at the kids, she steeled herself to enter the lion's den.

The only consolation was that Jamison was a true

gentleman. No matter how bad things had gotten between Jamison and her, he still stood up for her when his mother started in with her power plays— such as her insensitive queries about why Olivia wasn't pregnant yet and her attempts to pressure them into selling the house in Boston.

For the past year—since it had become clear that Jamison had garnered enough support to be considered a viable candidate for his party's nomination for a future presidential race—Helen Mallory had been turning up the pressure for Jamison to claim his birthright and move up to the family home in the Berkshires. Olivia knew it was a posturing on Helen's part, a way of positioning herself as close to her influential son's inner circle as possible. If the future president of the United States lived with her, in *her* house— because if she and Jamison moved in it didn't mean Helen would move out—then she would have an even better chance at having his ear and an even stronger chance at asserting her considerable influence, much in the same way she'd done with her late husband.

Stanhope Manor had been in the Mallory family for seven generations. It had always been, passed down to the oldest son. At thirty-nine, Jamison was still young, and would have plenty of time to enjoy the place with his own family, just as he and his five younger brothers had when they were growing up.

Despite how much Olivia wanted to uphold the Mallory legacy, she wasn't in a hurry to move out of the city into the rambling, eleven-bedroom, twenty-two-thousand-square-foot mansion until she could give her husband a son—or a daughter—who would carry on the tradition. What was the point without a family to fill the rambling house?

At least in Boston Olivia had her family and her volunteer work. One thing she did not need was further isolation.

Nor did she need—or want—to live with her mother-in-law. Especially with Jamison spending so much time in Washington. That living arrangement would surely prove to be a ticking time bomb ready to explode.

Residing in Boston meant Helen was a safe two hours away in the Berkshires. Long distance, it was more difficult for her to remind Olivia that she and Jamison had yet to gift the family with children. Except for the occasional obligatory phone call, Helen mostly ignored Olivia, saving the pregnancy barbs for personal delivery. For times such as this.

Olivia braced herself at the thought.

It hurt that she and Jamison had confided in her about their fertility struggles, yet Helen publicly persecuted them as if their childlessness were a choice. Sometimes Olivia had to summon every ounce of strength to keep from tossing Helen's barbs and patronizing tone right back at her. But out of respect for her husband, Olivia bit her tongue.

To Jamison's credit, he fully understood how painful it would be to live with his mother. Despite how he longed to move into the house in which he'd grown up, he always sided with Olivia, refusing to let Helen bully them into moving and demanding she lay off when her pregnancy digs got out of hand.

The valet opened Olivia's door and helped her step out of the Jaguar. Jamison walked around the car and took her hand, expecting her to play along. To put on a happy face and pretend they were the perfect couple with the perfect marriage.

"Are you okay?" he asked as they climbed the steps to the porch.

"Truthfully?" She slanted him a look. "No, I'm not."

His face fell, as if her words had knocked the wind out of him, but before he could say anything, the elaborately carved wooden front doors swung open and a uniformed doorman greeted them.

"Merry Christmas, sir, madam."

Ever the politician, Jamison flashed his famous smile. "Merry Christmas."

Olivia managed a polite nod. She didn't recognize the man at the door. He wasn't part of the small band of live-in staff employed by Jamison's mother. He was obviously among the extra help she'd hired for the holidays. Like a steadfast queen clinging to her castle, she'd remained in the house after Jamison's father died and all six boys had moved out to begin their own lives.

"Mrs. Mallory is in the great room. Follow me, please."

"Thank you, but that's not necessary," said Jamison. "I grew up in this house. I know the way."

The doorman stood back and motioned Jamison and Olivia onward. "Very well, sir. Happy holidays."

Their footsteps sounded on the marble floor. The place had a museumlike air that inspired silence. As they made their way down the long, arched hallway toward the great room at the back of the house, neither said a word.

Instead, Olivia let her gaze stray over the elaborate paintings lining the walls. Generations of Mallorys dating as far back as the Revolutionary War hung in grand, gilded frames. Their eyes seemed to follow Olivia and Jamison as they passed. Though she'd experienced this sensation many times, today it was eerie and a little unnerving. She shifted her gaze straight ahead, focusing on the crown molding at the end of the passageway.

In the great room, a harpist strummed Christmas

carols from her post in the corner. Her angelic music was barely audible above the crowd that was at least seventy-five strong. A giant Christmas tree stood in front of the large picture windows on the west wall that looked out over the snow-covered back lawn with its beautifully frozen pond. In the distance, the mountains painted a breathtaking picture. A roaring fire blazed in the oversize fireplace. The room was a little stuffy with all the people milling about talking, laughing and filling plates with fancy hors d'oeuvres that had been laid out on an antique trestle table that stretched nearly the entire length of the wall opposite the windows.

In the center of the crowded room, Helen Mallory was holding court, talking to her loyal subjects who were dutifully gathered around her. Her platinum hair, as white as new-fallen snow, was teased into a meringuelike coiffure. Her white cashmere suit and plethora of diamonds brought to mind the term "Ice Queen." As if sensing their presence, she looked up as Jamison and Olivia approached.

"Darlings, there you are," she said. Her drink sloshed as she raised her glass toward them. "I was beginning to think you'd never arrive." It was barely noon and judging by the glass Helen held like a scepter, she'd bypassed the traditional Christmas

Day pomegranate mimosas and had dived headfirst into the martinis. Depending on how many she'd had, they could be in for a bumpy ride.

Jamison bent down and kissed Helen's cheek.

"Merry Christmas, Mother. You're looking… well. We would've been here sooner, but last night my flight in from D.C. was delayed, and I didn't get home until after three."

Helen held out a diamond-laden hand to her daughter-in-law.

"Merry Christmas, dear." She looked Olivia up and down with disapproving eyes. "You're looking beautiful, as always. But awfully thin. I was so hoping you would've plumped up by now."

Helen pulled her hand from Olivia's and patted her daughter-in-law's flat stomach.

Trying to ignore the uncomfortable stares from the others gathered around them, Olivia took special care to keep her smile firmly in place. Especially since she had a feeling of what was coming next— right in front of everyone.

Olivia did a mental countdown. *Three, two, one—*

"When on earth are you going to give me a grandchild?"

Right on schedule.

"You do know that Payton is pregnant again, don't you?" Helen slurred the words.

Olivia fought back a sudden rush of emotions that brought with them the stinging threat of tears.

Payton. The wife of Jamison's younger brother, Grant. The perfect, fertile daughter-in-law. One only need talk about pregnancy in the vicinity of Payton and she got knocked up.

"Mother, don't start." Jamison's voice was flat.

Helen sighed and dismissed him with a curt wave of martini, diamonds and bloodred nails. The gesture sent a wave of gin sloshing over the side of her glass, leaving a wet spot on her white suit. She seemed not to notice.

"I'm not *starting* anything," she slurred. "I'm simply finding it terribly ironic that Olivia's father is one of the nation's leading fertility experts— Gerald Armstrong, of the Armstrong Institute—yet they're still not pregnant. I just don't understand." Helen directed her words to the others, spouting off as if this weren't a deeply private issue, acting as if Olivia and Jamison weren't standing right there.

Every fiber in Olivia's body went numb and she had to inhale sharply and bite the insides of her cheeks to keep from defending herself. Because what was the point?

Helen was drunk. Again. Come to think of it, Helen always said what was on her mind and seemed to get more brazenly outspoken with each passing year. Her drinking was also out of control, and the family seemed to be in complete denial about it.

It wasn't Olivia's place to say anything about her mother-in-law's imbibing, but these barbs…they were inexcusable. Talking as if Olivia's father were a banker refusing to lend money rather than seeing it for the intensely painful, sensitive—and private— issue that it was.

"Mother, stop it," Jamison insisted.

Normally, when Helen started with her polite bullying, Olivia didn't let the woman's barbs get to her—but today Olivia felt vulnerable. Fragile, almost.

So, when Jamison put an arm around her and locked gazes with his mother, Olivia sank into him. Against her will, her body responded to her husband's offer of solidarity and protection.

Despite what had transpired earlier, she was glad that at least he was taking her side, as he always did.

At least that hadn't changed.

Before Helen could say anything else, the uncomfortable standoff was interrupted by a ringing voice.

"Merry Christmas, all!" Payton waddled over to them, her freckled cheeks rosy and her baby bump looking much more pronounced in the holly-green velvet maternity dress than it should for a woman five months' pregnant. Of course, it was her fourth pregnancy.

Fourth baby in four-and-a-half years. Olivia swallowed the lump of sad envy that had burned in her throat until it slid down, settling like a hot coal in the pit of her barren belly.

"Payton, darling." Helen stood and pulled her favorite daughter-in-law into a gentle embrace. "How are you feeling, love?"

Payton pushed an auburn curl off her forehead, then beamed and rested her hands on her swollen belly. "I've never felt better."

Helen held her at arm's length, taking in her entire being. "It shows. You are positively radiant."

Payton preened. "I always feel my best when I'm pregnant."

Of course she did.

Lucky for her since she was *always* pregnant. Resentment flared inside Olivia. It seemed like Payton and Grant produced a child to commemorate each wedding anniversary.

"Here, sit, sit. Next to me. Get off your feet." Helen returned to her seat on the sofa and patted the cushion beside her.

"Well, Mom, we have been in the car all morning." She braced her right hand on the small of her back, which made her stomach stick out all the more. "But I guess I could sit a while longer while we catch up."

"You know, if you keep giving me grandchildren at this rate, I'm going to have to move you up here to Stanhope Manor so that there's a place big enough to house all of you under one roof. Jamison doesn't seem to have any interest in the place."

Helen shot a pointed look at her son as Payton planted herself next to her mother-in-law.

"It would be wonderful to live with you up here. If you keep talking like that, we just might take you up on it."

Olivia glanced at Jamison, who was wearing an *over-my-dead-body* look on his face. She had a hunch that his sour expression wasn't simply a remnant of his mother's earlier indelicate blurting, but had more to do with the threat of his younger brother's status-hungry wife bumping him out of his birthright with her pregnant belly.

Maybe, for once, Payton's selfish antics could actually help Olivia by making Jamison change his mind about holding off on having children. Even so, it seemed unlikely that an army of children could keep Helen at bay if they moved in with her.

Payton must have sensed Olivia staring because she smiled up at Jamison and Olivia and said, "It's been a long time. How are the two of you?"

They made small talk for a few moments until Grant entered with an infant seat in one hand, a toddler on the opposite hip and their oldest boy trailing behind him. Grant flashed his trademark toothy, white Mallory smile, greeting everyone as he walked over to kiss his mother's cheek.

Grant had been a latecomer to politics, winning a New Hampshire congressional seat just last year. He and Jamison had always been competitive, but when it came to politics, there was an unwritten agreement that Jamison was the one who would make a bid for the White House. After he'd had his go, then, if Grant was game, it was all his.

Olivia wondered if the same accord applied to Stanhope Manor or if Helen would seriously offer the home to Grant and Payton—even as a strategic move to force Jamison and Olivia's hand. On top of everything else, the thought was more than Olivia could deal with. So she pushed it out of her mind, vowing only to worry about it if and when the crisis came up.

"Merry Christmas, son," Helen said to Grant. "And where's your nanny? Surely you didn't give her this week off? Now more than ever your wife needs the extra hands to help her."

Grant and Payton had imported a woman named Ingrid from Sweden to help with the kids. Payton took pride in flaunting her Swedish nanny, so it was a surprise when Grant said, "She went home for the holidays."

Helen shot Payton an alarmed glance. "Oh, you poor dear. However will you manage?"

Olivia was delighted to fall off of Helen's radar as Payton dutifully played the martyred mommy, regaling her audience with details of how it would indeed be a challenge, but that she would somehow get by.

Anger and shame rose in Olivia's throat like bile, as she moved as far away from Payton as possible.

As the day progressed, Helen wasn't the only one driving the baby train. Payton and her brood—and pregnant belly—drew inevitable comparisons and incessant questions from friends and relatives about why Jamison and Olivia weren't keeping up with his younger brothers.

If Olivia had been in a certain frame of mind, she would've taken offense at their questions. Asking a couple about when they were going to have a baby was not so far off from quizzing them about their sex life. It was a private matter. Didn't people understand that?

Obviously it took sex for pregnancy to happen.

Unless the couple went the in vitro route, as Jamison and Olivia well knew. They'd tried to conceive the usual way, and when that failed, they'd opted for in vitro.

The hormones to help Olivia produce more eggs for harvesting had wreaked havoc with her physical well-being, causing headaches and mood swings and overall malaise. She and Jamison had ended up fighting, so much so that they'd decided to separate.

The thought of how something as wonderful as having a baby could create such turmoil in a marriage was beyond Olivia.

She wished Jamison could understand it was the side effects of the hormones that had caused their problems. Not the possibility that their marriage was unstable. And certainly not the act of having a baby and building their family. Looking at it rationally, she could understand his hesitation. She just wished he could believe that it would be different when they tried again.

Because it would be.

This time she knew what to expect. This time she would be prepared.

A new doctor had recently joined the Armstrong Fertility Institute. Chance Demetrios was one of the leading fertility research specialists in the world. Her brother Paul had hired him away from a teaching hospital in San Francisco. Olivia had seen him once, just before she and Jamison decided on the trial separation, and she hadn't followed up when he'd said there was a slim chance she could get pregnant. Slim, but a chance nonetheless. Since the pain of their separation was so fresh, Olivia's mindset made her question the point of following up if her husband wasn't on board.

But now, especially as she watched Payton, Olivia was looking at things differently. Suddenly, there was an urgency. There was no time to waste. Maybe it was Jamison's sudden hesitation, but Olivia was feeling her full twenty-nine years. She certainly wasn't getting any younger. Maybe, if Jamison wasn't willing to cooperate, it was time to take maters into her own hands—even if it meant getting pregnant without her husband's blessing.

After all, once she was carrying his child, he'd come around.

Wouldn't he?

Jamison retreated into the library with his glass of wine. As a kid, he'd always enjoyed the solitude of the room—the built-in mahogany bookcases and never-ending stacks of books felt like comfortable old friends. When life overwhelmed him or he had a problem that needed sorting out, he'd come here, grab a book and sit in the window seat. Sometimes he'd lose himself in a classic. More often than not, he'd lose himself in his thoughts as he gazed at the panoramic view of the mountains that stretched like a grand painting framed by the horizon of the backyard.

Tonight, the moonless sky hid the mountains as

if nature had drawn a black velvet curtain. So he bypassed the window seat, placed another log on the dying fire and settled into one of the leather club chairs in front of the hearth.

It was late. He and Olivia really should head home soon, but he needed a few minutes alone to gather his thoughts before they climbed into the car and endured another long, silent journey.

He didn't blame her for being mad at him. It seemed that since he'd been home he'd committed one seemingly thoughtless blunder after another. He'd even managed to blow it with Olivia this evening after the friends had gone and the party shifted into a mode of opening Christmas presents and snapping family photos. Oh, she hadn't said it straight out—in fact she'd barely said more than, "Thank you," but the flash of confusion in her eyes had been unmistakable when she'd opened her gift from him and had seen the gaudy cocktail ring that was not in the least bit her style—and several sizes too big to boot.

Crunched for time, he'd asked his mother to pick up a gift for Olivia from him—jewelry, something nice, of course. "You know Olivia. Pick out something she'd like."

When his tiny, pearl-wearing wife had opened the jewelers box and pulled out the multi-colored boulder of a cocktail ring, he'd wanted to snatch it back and claim that there had been a mistake. On her delicate hand, it looked like a wild, golf-ball-size piece of stained glass; certainly nothing he would've ever picked out for her. And that had been obvious. He hadn't shopped for his wife. She'd been well aware of that since the ring had his mother's signature written all over it.

For someone who prided himself on intelligence, he felt pretty dumb for entrusting his mother, of all people, to shop for Olivia. That blunder, on top of the fact that it probably hadn't been the best time to tell Olivia he wanted to hold off on getting pregnant. Not on the heels of disappointing her with the change of plans for Christmas week. But thoughtlessly, he'd done it. It had slipped out as they'd talked earlier that morning. They'd digressed back into the dubious tug of war over commitment and priorities, which went from bad to worse when he'd broken the news that he had to leave because he had to play host to the visiting ambassador. She hadn't taken it well. No matter that a lot was riding on this meeting, and if he pulled it off it would be a major coup, a feather in his political cap.

The flames crackled in the fireplace.

The ridiculous ring felt like a third strike in a game he was already losing. He was between a rock and a hard place. Olivia knew their life would be this way and if he did make that run for the White House in 2016, not only did they need to find solidarity in their marriage, they had to be a solid twosome before they could add to their family.

Still, it didn't mean he loved her any less. As a matter of fact, he was standing firm on his position to hold off starting a family because he loved her. Children added a whole different dynamic to a marriage, and he wasn't so naive to believe that a child would fix something that was broken. He'd seen plenty of evidence to support that fact as he'd watched his parents' marriage come apart under the pressure of public office and the weight of lies and deception. The only reason his mother and father hadn't divorced was because of his father's untimely death.

Well-shrouded secrets and, of course, the soft focus of layers of decades had allowed his mother the privilege of playing the well-respected, grieving widow of a political hero—a senator who would've been president had his life not been tragically snuffed out. But as the oldest of six boys, Jamison had gotten a first-hand look at the real life behind the gossamer curtain that cloaked political power couple, Judson and Helen Mallory.

Jamison sipped his cabernet. He was nothing like his old man, aside from carrying on his father's political legacy. In fact, Jamison had consciously tried to stay clear of the womanizing and scandal that not only plagued the Mallory name, but had driven his mother to the bottle and kept his family life in constant upheaval. If he'd gleaned nothing else from observing his parents' destructive relationship, it was that he knew children could not fix a rocky marriage.

Children simply got caught in the cross fire.

Behind him, the library door creaked open. A slant of light yawned across the wall then disappeared as the door shut. Jamison turned around, hoping Olivia had decided to join him. Instead, his mother stood there, tall and proud and expressionless. Her angular features were rendered even sharper by the dim amber glow of the fire. She glided across the room and slid into the chair next to him.

He could feel her gaze on him, as palpable as the heat of the fire at his feet.

"I thought I'd find you here," she said. "Anytime you had something on your mind, you'd always hide in here."

"I'm not hiding, Mother. Simply enjoying the solitude."

"Don't try to fool me." She shifted in her seat, angling her knees toward him, crossing her legs at the ankles, folding her hands in her lap. "You of all people wouldn't leave a party unless you had something weighing on your mind."

Jamison took a slow sip of wine, buying time. Interesting that his mother had been drinking most of the day and she still had the uncanny ability to read him. Of course, his retreating into solitude had probably been a big tip-off. Rather than slipping off, he probably should've rallied Olivia and simply headed for home. But he'd wanted to think, wanted to find common ground on which they could meet as they drove home.

"I'm exhausted," he said. "Thanks to work and the weather, it hasn't exactly been a jolly holiday."

He set his wine on the end table next to his seat, got up and stoked the fire. It flared, spit and crackled as he turned the log.

"I can see that you're exhausted," she said to his back. "You haven't been yourself all day. I do wish you would stay the night and get a fresh start tomorrow. Grant, Payton and the kids are staying."

He returned the poker to its brass stand. "Thank you, but we can't stay. I have an early flight tomorrow. We really should head for home."

A chain of silent seconds stretched between them.

"You always did love this room," she said. "It's too bad you can't enjoy it more often."

He shrugged and glanced at her. "I don't even get to enjoy my own home as often as I'd like."

A flash as hot as the glint of a flame lit her eyes. "Why are you going back to Washington so soon?"

He disengaged her gaze and turned his attention back to the dancing fire. "An unexpected meeting came up."

"A meeting. During Christmas week." There was a goading, knowing tone to her voice, as if she'd caught him in a lie, but was willing to keep his secret.

Despite the pause in conversation, Jamison didn't elaborate.

"The one-size-fits-all excuse. That's the one your father used to use all the time. 'I have a meeting.' And how was I supposed to know differently?"

"Mom, don't."

He hadn't realized how badly she was slurring her words. He really didn't want his mother to string together all of his father's flaws and illuminate them like tawdry lights on a tainted family tree.

"The wife never knows until it's too late. When she finds out, all she can do to save face is go on pretending she's none the wiser. It's a miserable life, Jamison. Don't put Olivia through that. I hardly think she's strong enough to cope."

Was she implying that he was having an affair? It rankled him. Even so, he wasn't going to defend himself against something he had no intention of doing. Besides, she was drunk and probably wouldn't remember the conversation in the morning.

"This is your house, Jamison. I know Olivia doesn't want to live here, but she needs to understand that Mallory men…well, affairs just seem to be a way of life. If you move in here, I can help her cope. I can help her understand that it's just something Mallory men do."

He held up his hand. "Mother, stop. I am not having an affair. I have no intention of having an affair. I love my wife."

Helen threw back her head and guffawed a most unladylike sound. "Oh, Jamison, you can level with me. I'm not going to tell her."

She was talking utter nonsense. It was definitely time to go.

He stood and walked toward the door.

Helen's body swiveled as she followed him with her gaze.

"Where are you going?" she demanded.

"Home, Mother. It's late, but I thank you for a wonderful evening. Merry Christmas."

"Jamison, don't walk away from me. I need to ask you a question."

He stopped, his hand on the doorknob.

"Seven generations of Mallorys have lived here, son. How much longer are you planning on allowing that woman to deny you what's yours? You need to set your wife straight. Tell her it's time."

"It's not time, and it won't be until and unless Olivia is ready."

Helen made a clucking sound and stood up, wobbling as she did.

"You're just like your father, Jamison, always letting a pretty face cloud your judgment and sway your decision. Stand up and be a man, son."

Jamison shook his head. "Oh, Mother, what you don't understand is that the main difference between Dad and me is that I am being a man. The pretty face that influences me is my wife. I'm sorry he never showed you the same courtesy."

Chapter Three

Where do you go when you can't go home?

Back to the purgatory of Washington, D.C., Jamison thought. Even though it was the last place he wanted to be.

But duty called. Olivia should understand that.

Jamison stood in the dining room of his house, pouring himself a stiff glass of scotch.

It was nearly nine o'clock. The tense ride home from his mother's had mirrored the mostly silent drive up. Olivia was upset, and he understood why—on so many levels. The only problem was there was nothing he could do about it.

He carried his drink back into the living room where Olivia waited for him, perched on the edge of the white living room sofa, anxiously fidgeting with the too-big cocktail ring he'd given her for Christmas, twisting it around and around on her index finger.

He'd been so bogged down with work he'd hadn't had time to shop. His mom had offered to pick out something nice for Olivia, something tasteful, yet lavish. Why hadn't Helen opted for a bracelet or a necklace? No. Not a necklace because that would've paled in comparison to the diamond necklace Grant had had designed for Payton—one obscenely large diamond representing each child they'd had together. Payton, of course, had been very quick to notice and point out that the design provided plenty of room for endless additions. A sudden rush of guilt washed over Jamison as he remembered Olivia opening her gift that was noticeably too large and, really, more his mother's style than her own.

So maybe his wife was partially right. Maybe they needed to reevaluate, reprioritize. In fact, that's exactly what they would do right after this diplomatic visit was over. Then after they'd worked on themselves, they could revisit babies and parenthood.

"Are you sure I can't get you anything?" he asked

as he walked over to the fireplace. He set his glass on the mantel and picked up the poker to stir the fire he'd lit when they arrived.

"No, thank you," she said. "I'm fine."

But she wasn't *fine.* She was looked anything but *fine,* and he almost couldn't stand it. He plugged in the Christmas tree lights and dimmed the rheostat, hoping to gain a more romantic atmosphere that would lift her mood and turn the tide in their favor for once.

"I'm sorry the ring is too big. The jeweler can resize it."

"I guess your mother didn't know my size?" The corners of her mouth turned up, but the smile didn't reach her eyes.

"You know I didn't plan on having to go back to Washington so soon," Jamison said. "No more than I planned on spending Christmas Eve at the mercy of the weather."

Inhaling a weary breath, she said, "I thought that story was strictly reserved for the family's benefit." The words weren't sharp or nasty. More disappointed...or, worse yet, defeated.

For a moment, neither of them said a word.

"I'm just tired of begging for your time, Jamison," she said as if answering his thoughts.

"Honey, you knew when you married me that sometimes my job would preempt pleasure."

Even the pleasure of making love to his wife. What a pity that they were arguing rather than doing exactly that in the small amount of time they had together.

She simply shook her head.

"I don't want to fight, Jamison. Not tonight. It's just too exhausting." She stood.

"Where are you going?"

"I'm going to take a bath, and then I'm going to bed. What time is your flight tomorrow?"

"Nine o'clock. The ambassador arrives at one."

She nodded. "I'm sure the weather will cooperate for you."

As she brushed past him, he was enveloped in a light floral breeze—the scent of her. He longed to reach out and pull her back, pull her into his arms. Because it felt as if every time she walked away from him, she was that much closer to walking out the door.

Olivia turned the bathtub faucet on as hot as it could go, and went to lie down while the tub filled.

The bedroom was spacious enough to comfortably house a king-size bed, antique armoire and dresser. There was also a sitting area with a couch, two chintz-covered wingback chairs and a coffee table arranged around a good-size fireplace.

They'd moved into the massive three-story brick house about five years ago. At the time, even though they'd been married two years, they still acted as if they were on their honeymoon—so much in love, dreaming and planning for the future.

Olivia rolled over on her side and hugged a silk throw pillow to her middle.

She couldn't remember when their relationship had taken such a bad turn. Or maybe it wasn't a turn so much as they'd simply lost themselves somewhere along the way.

Funny how they were still fooling even those closest to them. Everyone looked at them in their fancy dream house and thought they had it all—the perfect American dream.

Yet, here she was on Christmas, feeling further away from her husband than she ever had, rather than putting back together the marriage they'd secretly taken apart. Her head throbbed and her heart ached and she closed her eyes for a moment, trying to block a pain that wasn't physical as much as emotional.

Obviously, there was no reasoning with Jamison once he'd made up his mind. But no matter what happened between them, she was bound and determined to have the baby she so desperately wanted.

Which meant since things were so uncertain

between them, she'd better get pregnant as soon as possible, while their friends, families—and Jamison's constituents—still believed they were the happy couple.

The ache of regret deepened as her heart bucked against the thought of her marriage ending. She wasn't trying to be negative, just the realist she'd become over the years she'd been married to Jamison. Another possibility niggled at her. If…no, *when* she got pregnant, it would be an insurance policy for her marriage. After all, when Jamison made his bid for the presidency, he certainly wouldn't win any votes if his constituents learned he'd divorced his wife when she was pregnant.

She sat up stock straight in her bed. She couldn't think that way. Nothing negative, only positive, good thoughts for the baby.

Across the room, a blinking light on the telephone caught her eye. Absently, she got to her feet, padded over to the phone and pressed the button to check the messages.

"Merry Christmas, Olivia and Jamison," a male and female voice rang out in unison. It was her brother, Paul, and his fiancée, Ramona. Hearing their voices brought an involuntary smile to Olivia's lips.

"We missed you last night at Mom and Dad's." Now it was only her big brother's voice on the message. "I just wanted to wish you well. Please call when you get back from the Berkshires."

Even though she and Paul were as different as night and day, they'd always been close. In fact, she was much closer to him than she was to her younger sister, Lisa, and Paul's twin Derek. Her three siblings were career-minded, following in their father's footsteps, running the institute, while Olivia had no interest in the family business. All she'd ever wanted to be was a supportive wife and good mother—to invest in a family of her own. She wasn't unambitious—making their home and supporting Jamison in his career made her happy.

Or at least that's what had made her happy once upon a time.

Now, the only way she could recapture that contentment was to have a baby. To accomplish that, she needed to talk to her doctor, Chance Demetrios, as soon as possible.

As the medical director at the Armstrong Institute, Paul would know Chance's schedule. Plus, hearing Paul's voice would be like an infusion of sunshine, and the voice of reason, to boot. While she couldn't confide in him about her marital woes—she couldn't risk trusting *anyone* with that personal information—she *could* trust him with the secret that she'd decided to move ahead with the artificial insemination.

She turned off the tub, then walked back into the bedroom, settled into one of the wingback chairs, and dialed his number with a nervous hand.

Chapter Four

Jamison climbed the stairs toward the master bedroom. It was Christmas, for God's sake. He couldn't let her go to bed mad. He hated that things had digressed to this point. Before he went to bed he had to try and apologize, because the last thing he wanted was to leave for Washington with things like this. They were supposed to be gaining ground in their relationship, not losing it.

As he raised his hand to knock on the door, he thought he heard a voice—Olivia's voice. Was she talking to someone?

Her tone was light and happy—a bit giddy, in

fact—though he couldn't make out what she was saying until he got to the door and heard her say, "I have to see him as soon as possible. If not, I think I'm going to die."

See who?

He resisted the urge to eavesdrop and rapped lightly on the door. It wasn't just the way Olivia flinched when she turned and saw him standing there, or the way she stiffened when he walked in, but it was the way her voice changed that gave him pause.

"I have to go," she said. "I'll talk to you soon." With that, she abruptly ended the call.

They looked at each other for a moment. When it became clear that she wasn't going to offer any information, he asked, "Who was that?"

"Nobody." She spit the word too fast, stood too quickly and crossed to the bed, aimlessly smoothing wrinkles from the comforter.

"Nobody?" His tone was a little sharper than he'd intended, but something was up. She wasn't talking to *nobody.* "It sounded like somebody to me."

She ducked her head, refusing to look him in the eye. He fought the urge to cross to her and take her face in his hands and force her to look at him. He'd never been a suspicious man, but then again, his wife had always been very open and sharing. They'd never harbored secrets. This definitely smelled like a secret.

He heaved an exasperated, full-body sigh that was laced with anger and resentment.

She must have sensed his mood.

"It was Paul." Her words were flat with a terse edge. "He called to wish us a Merry Christmas."

"He called? I didn't hear the phone ring."

She squinted at him, shooting poisonous darts with her eyes. "He and Ramona called earlier and left a message while we were at your mother's house. I returned their call. Any other questions?"

Yes, he had question, such as how she could be so light and giddy one moment and then turn so cold and guarded when he walked into the room. And who was this man she so desperately needed to see?

Jamison knew his wife well enough to sense that something wasn't quite right. Something that stretched beyond the baby issue. Something that she wasn't telling him. Even though he might not get it out of her tonight, he'd find out eventually…one way or another.

At seven o'clock the next morning, Olivia and Jamison sat at the dining room table eating poached eggs on whole wheat toast, which Olivia had prepared. A peace offering after the run-in last night. Actually, it was an olive branch after a reunion that had more closely resembled a train wreck than the rekindling of the relationship they'd both wanted.

She tried to keep her mood light. She shouldn't have been so defensive last night, but she wasn't sure how much he'd heard after surprising her while she was talking to Paul, who'd told her that Chance Demetrios was indeed in town this week. Jamison had walked in as Paul was explaining that Chance had planned to use the week while the institute was closed to catch up on some paperwork. Paul had promised to have Chance call her as soon as possible.

Jamison was quietly subdued this morning, and as each minute passed without him asking questions or flat out telling her what he'd heard, she relaxed a little more, allowing herself to believe that her plan was still securely in place.

She hated keeping secrets from him. Frankly, she wasn't used to doing so and obviously wasn't very good at it—as evidenced by her defensive display last night, when she was tired and emotionally drained.

Now that she was rested, it was sinking in that Jamison's having to return to Washington this morning might actually be a blessing in disguise. With her husband away, she wouldn't have to lie to him about her decision to pursue the in vitro fertilization on her own.

Rather than looking at it as a lie of omission, she chose to think of it in terms of asking for forgiveness later rather than asking for permission right now.

"Breakfast was delicious, as always," Jamison said after he swallowed the last bite. "I'll try to get home by New Year's Eve. I'll call you tonight and let you know how things are shaping up."

Olivia nodded and sipped her herbal tea. "That sounds like a plan."

He smiled at her and reached out and covered her free hand with his. "You do know how much I love you, don't you?"

The earnestness in his voice tugged at Olivia's heart, and when she looked at him, the depth of emotion in his blue eyes nearly took away her breath.

"Yes, Jamison, I do. And I love you, too."

He leaned in, and his lips brushed hers. A whisper of a kiss so unexpected, it made her stiffen and brace her hands against his chest. But then, like sweet ice cream melting in the heat of the sun, she softened and kissed him back, slowly at first.

His mouth tasted of grapefruit juice and coffee and that indefinable flavor that was uniquely him— something for which, she realized suddenly and desperately, she'd been hungering—no, starving—for far too long. She didn't want him to stop. So she slid her arms around his neck and opened her mouth, deepening the kiss, and fisting her hands into his shirt, pulling their bodies closer.

Maybe he'd changed his mind and would stay with her in Boston rather than going back to D.C. The thought made her heart pound. On one level, she relished the feeling of being alive again, having her husband touch her and respond to her touching him back. Yet on a deeper plane, she sought refuge in the shelter of his arms, their kisses healing the hurt they'd both suffered during their time apart.

At that moment, she knew that they would be okay. They had to be. Because there was no alternative. Plain and simple, she simply couldn't imagine life without him. She intended to tell him so by leading him up to the bedroom, but the ringing phone preempted her physical love note.

"That's probably the driver," Jamison whispered. "Wow, he's early." He kissed her again, trailing his lips down her neck, but even that didn't stop the incessant ringing. Finally, holding her, his forehead pressed against hers, he sighed. "I hate it that I have to go. I'm sorry. It's not what I planned." He gathered her hands in his. "Would you mind answering and telling him I'll be right out?"

Olivia answered the phone on the fourth ring, just before it switched over to the answering service.

"Hello?"

"Good morning," said a deep male voice. "May I speak to Olivia, please?"

"This is she."

"It's Chance Demetrios. Your brother, Paul, asked me to call you this morning about setting up another appointment."

Olivia's heart slammed against her breastbone.

She glanced toward the kitchen door for signs of Jamison, then lowered her voice and started walking toward the office where she could close the door and not risk her husband overhearing. "Thank you for calling, Dr. Demetrios, especially since the institute is closed for the holidays."

"It's not a problem. I'm working through the holiday. I noticed that your file indicates that we called and ultimately sent you a letter several months ago asking you to come in for further tests. Did you receive that letter?"

Olivia swallowed a twinge of guilt. "Yes, Dr. Demetrios, I did. For a while, we were thinking of delaying starting our family, but that's no longer the case. We're ready to move ahead."

"Wonderful," said Demetrios. "If you're available, I can see you tomorrow."

"That would be lovely. I must apologize for not following up sooner."

"Well, I was reviewing your file a moment ago and I think I may have some new insight to what is causing your problems."

Olivia's heart leaped. "Does that mean you know how to fix what's wrong with me?"

There was a pause on the other end of the line, and Olivia couldn't tell if that meant the doctor had good news or bad.

"We'll need to run some more tests, but we can do that and talk about it tomorrow when you come in."

After wheeling his bag into the living room, Jamison came back into the kitchen to kiss his wife goodbye. She wasn't there.

"Olivia," he called. "I have to go, the car's waiting."

No answer.

He fought back a surge of impatience. *Calm down.* Things had finally started getting back on track. He didn't want to ruin it now. But where had she disappeared to, knowing that he had to leave?

Rather than stew over it, Jamison decided to signal to the driver that he'd be out in a moment. Maybe by that time Olivia would reappear.

Yet when he opened the front door and looked out into the impossibly sunny cold morning to busy

Commonwealth Avenue, the car wasn't there. Perplexed, he stepped back inside and closed the door. Then, as if driven by a sixth sense, he followed his intuition down the hall to the study. He stopped outside the door when he heard Olivia talking in hushed tones.

"That sounds absolutely perfect," she said. "But may I call you back? I can't really talk right now."

At that moment, the doorbell rang. The car, no doubt. Jamison walked soundlessly down the hall so that Olivia wouldn't see him and ducked back into the living room.

When she finally joined him a moment later, he patted his pockets. "I think I forgot something. Would you tell the driver I'll be right out?"

"Sure."

Jamison went into the spare bedroom where he'd spent the past two nights, picked up the phone extension, and pressed the record for the caller ID log.

The name that appeared was Chance Demetrios. The doctor that she'd seen only once—or at least only one time that he was aware of.

All sorts of questions raced through his mind: Why was he calling her now? Was this the man who, last night, she'd sounded so anxious to see?

Feeling threatened on a number of levels, when he got to the front door, Jamison pulled Olivia into a tight embrace—and again he kissed her as if he really meant it.

So what if he was being territorial. He had good reason. He loved her and he couldn't stand the thought of her keeping secrets from him or worse yet, turning to another man when she should be confiding in him. He'd given her too much space. Been too busy. Too wrapped up in work, his thoughts focused firmly on the future presidential election. Even so, he still hoped she'd turn to him before she ran to someone else. Even if the man was her doctor.

It was a shame it took something like this to remind him that they belonged together.

His lips found her earlobe, her jaw, her neck and he trailed possessive kisses down to her collarbone. He knew he had to stop. The driver was waiting and if he didn't stop now, he'd sweep his wife up in his arms and take her upstairs to their bed and prove exactly how much he loved her, like he should've done the minute he got home on Christmas Eve.

"Jamison, you'd better go," she said breathlessly, breaking the contact.

She slid her hands from his shoulders down his arms and took his hands in hers.

There they stood, face-to-face, eye-to-eye—and the words just slipped out.

"Who was on the phone?"

Just like that, her face shuttered again, closing him out. Her eyes held the mysterious darkness of kept secrets.

"No one." She stepped away from him, opened the front door. The cold winter wind blew in, cutting him down to the core of his body.

"Well, I heard the phone ring and it wasn't the driver. Was it a wrong number? Your sister? The Salvation Army?"

She looked at him as if he was crazy. For a desperate, furious moment he felt he was stark, raving mad.

"None of the above," she insisted. "You're going to miss your flight if you don't go."

He looked at her closely. "You're keeping something from me."

"No, I'm not."

The protest came a little too quickly and fervently. The shuttered look on her face made it difficult for him to read her. That's why he was so taken aback when she reached up and cupped his jaw in her hand.

"I love you, Jamison. You just have to trust me, okay?"

Trust her? When she's obviously keeping something from me? Even so—

"I love you, too. Please don't ever forget it, okay?"

He gave her one last hug before he walked down the red brick steps and got into the car. As soon as the vehicle pulled away, he took out his BlackBerry and dialed Cameron McInerney, his aide.

"Good morning, Cameron. I need you to do a background check on a Dr. Chance Demetrios of Boston. Hire a P.I. if you need to. I want to know everything about this guy, every move he makes."

Jamison hung up the phone and slid it into the breast pocket of his coat. He stared out the window at the tall buildings of downtown Boston. It was his home, but this morning it felt so strange.

Soon enough he'd know if Dr. Demetrios was, indeed, *no one,* as Liv claimed…or if he was someone that Jamison needed to be concerned about.

Either way, he intended to discover exactly what his wife was keeping from him.

Chapter Five

The next day Olivia arrived at the institute early so that she could thank Paul for arranging her appointment with Chance Demetrios. True to form, he was back at work even though the institute was closed for the holidays for the rest of the week.

She rapped on his door. When he looked up, she wriggled her fingers at him.

"Hello, stranger," he said, rising from his desk and walking to meet her. He pulled her into a rib-crushing bear hug. When he let her go, he asked, "Where's Jamison?"

Olivia donned her best *happy wife* smile.

"He had to go back to D.C. yesterday." She shrugged. "I was disappointed, but I understand that duty calls. He hated to disrupt our plans. He's coming back next week, though."

When Paul started nodding, she realized she was babbling and stopped.

"So how are you?" he asked.

"I'm doing fine. I can't tell you how much I appreciate your help getting me an appointment with Dr. Demetrios today."

He waved it off. "Oh, it was nothing. Both Chance and I are here this week. So I figured it would be a good opportunity to get you in. Otherwise, he's pretty booked. Business is booming."

Paul smiled proudly as he motioned her to sit down. Her brother was the consummate workaholic. Even so, he used to be worse before his fiancée, Ramona Tate, came into his life. Before they met, he rarely took a day off. Ramona had been good for him in that respect, and it was wonderful to see him so happy. Not only that, her brother's love story was encouraging. His and Ramona's relationship had grown out of the worst sort of adversity when Paul's twin, Derek, had hired her without consulting either Paul or their sister, Lisa. Plus, Derek did not do a thorough background check. If he had, he would have discovered that Ramona was an investigative reporter intent on going undercover to write an unflattering exposé on the institute. Olivia was the only one of Gerald Armstrong's kids who had opted out of the family business. She just wasn't wired for business the way her brothers and sister were.

It was times like this that she was glad she'd followed her own path.

Olivia and her siblings had made their father proud by graduating from Harvard. But that's where the similarities ended. Instead of studying business and medicine, Olivia had majored in literature and minored in ballet. In fact, in her sophomore year she'd had the great honor of being tapped as one of Harvard Ballet's youngest assistant artistic directors. She'd spent her entire stint at Harvard performing with the company in which she'd taken such pride.

Even so, as her relationship with Jamison had become more serious, it had eventually eclipsed her love of dance and she'd given it up for marriage and a family of her own.

Despite her traditional values, she'd always danced to her own tune. Perhaps that was why she was having such a hard time letting Jamison dictate when they'd have children.

The situation with Ramona had caused a lot of family strain, and Olivia took heart in this perfect example of love conquering all. If her brother's re-

lationship could come up against such strife and
survive, surely Jamison could forgive her extreme
measures of starting their family. Because despite her
husband's belief otherwise, there was never a perfect
time to have a baby. She was sure Jamison would
understand that, once he held his child in his arms.

When Olivia got to Dr. Demetrios's office, she
was surprised when he asked her to come in and sit
down rather than having her change into a gown and
wait for him in one of the examination rooms.

She sat in a leather-upholstered chair across from
his desk, clenching her hands, nervous and giddy at
the same time.

"I'm glad you decided to come in, Mrs. Mallory."

He was a handsome man, and Olivia was surprised that a woman hadn't snatched him up by
now. Her mind did a quick inventory of single
friends who might a good match for him. The
single list grew shorter every year. Not surprising,
since Olivia and most of her friends were now
happily married.

Happily married.

The thought made Olivia shift in her seat as she
ignored the nagging voice that asked what she was
doing here alone if she was *happily married*.

"Please call me Olivia."

He smiled at her and pushed a wisp of dark hair off his forehead. "Certainly, Olivia."

He cleared his throat and for the flash of a second, she noticed a hint of something in his chocolate brown eyes that didn't bode well.

She tightened the grip on her hands, digging her fingernails into her palms.

"I don't quite know how to say this other than to come right out and say it, but your symptoms indicate that you might be having trouble conceiving because it's possible your body is going through early onset menopause."

His words rang in her ears.

"Menopause?" she heard herself utter. "But I'm only twenty-nine years old, Doctor. How can that be possible?"

He raked a hand across his handsome face as if this wasn't easy for him. "It's rare, but it does happen. The blood tests I did last time showed low levels of estradiol, which indicates your ovaries are starting to fail."

"You've known this for two months and you didn't tell me?" she asked as a burning salty sting in the back of her throat brought tears to her eyes and nearly choked her.

"I'm deeply sorry," he said. "I did try to contact you. My nurse even sent you a letter asking you to follow up with me, but you didn't respond. Because of patient confidentiality laws, I couldn't leave a more detailed message."

She'd received the vague letter that had asked her to set a follow-up appointment to discuss her test results. She'd thought it meant that he wanted to discuss which procedure they'd try next time and she hadn't followed through because of the trial separation.

How foolish she'd been thinking she had all the time in the world, that she could let nearly three months go by without making any effort to conceive. At least this further justified her being here today—her not mentioning to Jamison the meeting with Dr. Demetrios and making the decision to move ahead—all on her own.

"Do my brothers and sister know about this?" she asked. If they knew and hadn't told her she might never be able to forgive them.

"No, they don't know. Again, that's because of confidentiality laws."

Olivia swiped at a tear and Chance nudged a box of tissue toward her.

"But before, you said there was a slim chance that I could conceive."

"I'm sorry. That was before I received the test results."

Olivia swiped at the tears streaming down her face. It certainly wasn't the news she wanted to hear, especially with Jamison being so far away... She had to be strong and hear him out. One step at a time. She'd do everything he said she had to do to reverse this condition and then maybe that would be the answer to Jamison's and her fertility problems.

"As I'm sure you can understand, this comes as a total and complete shock, but I'm willing to do whatever needs to be done to reverse the situation. Please tell me, what's caused this and most importantly, what can we do to correct it?"

Chance shifted in his chair, his handsome face looking pained.

"It's hard to pin down the exact reason this has occurred, especially since there isn't a family history of it. But I do have to speculate that your low body weight may have been a contributor. Have you always been this thin, Olivia?"

Her weight had always been a sensitive subject. A war she'd battled in much the same way as some people battled excess weight. She'd always been naturally thin, but as a ballerina she was encouraged to be even thinner. *The thinner the better.* But even though ballet had been a big part of her life before she'd met Jamison, she would've given it up and gotten downright plump if she'd known her low weight was causing such harm.

Again, she choked back a rush of tears. "But my other question, Dr. Demetrios, is what do I have to do to reverse this condition?"

He looked stricken and Olivia knew what he was going to say before he said it. Even so, as the words, "I'm sorry, early onset menopause isn't reversible," spilled out of his mouth, Olivia's vision went white-hot and fuzzy around the edges. The walls were closing in—she had to get out of that office.

The next thing she knew, she found herself in the parking lot, huddled against the biting cold December wind, sobbing uncontrollably and fumbling in her purse for her keys.

As she pulled them out, Chance was standing beside her saying something about not letting her drive when she was so upset, but the words were so jumbled she couldn't quite be sure.

When he touched her arm, she nearly crumpled and fell into a heap of sobs and tears right there in the parking lot. Dr. Demetrios caught her in the nick of time and held her as she sobbed. But the feel of his strong arms around her made her long for Jamison. She jerked away from him, clicked the car door remote and tried to slide her slight frame into the driver's seat. Chance caught her arm and kept her from doing so.

"Olivia, you're too upset to drive." He'd chased after her without a jacket and he shivered against the cold. "Please come back inside until you can get a hold of yourself. It's cold out here and you really have no business driving right now."

Get a hold of myself?

She glared at him. He had just shattered her world with a single revelation. How was she supposed to *get a hold of herself* when she no longer had a foundation to stand on?

"I can't go back in there," she said through gritted teeth. "I'm not ready to tell my family about…" She took a deep breath. "About my condition. Not until I've had a chance to process it myself and discuss it with my husband."

Chance nodded.

"I understand. But I still can't let you drive right now. Let's walk over to the Coach House Diner just up the street. Then I'll take you home. We could get some coffee at the diner—"

"I don't drink coffee," she snapped, and immediately regretted it. Especially since he didn't bristle back at her. He remained calm, unfazed. His dark eyes were patient and kind.

"I'm sorry, Dr. Demetrios. It's just that…" Instinctively, almost protectively, she laced her hands over her belly.

He smiled his patient smile and nodded to let her know he understood.

"No apology necessary. You've received shattering news. What kind of a doctor would I be if I didn't cut you some slack? But as I said, I'd still like to discuss your options."

"I have options? The prognosis sounded pretty final."

"There are possibilities. I don't want to falsely raise your hopes, but this isn't the end of the line. If you'd prefer not to come back inside, let's go to the diner."

Olivia sucked in a breath. She was feeling markedly stronger now.

"I suppose I could go back to your office."

"Good, I'd put on a fresh pot of coffee just before you arrived and I'm dying for a cup. I'll steep you a cup of herbal tea and we'll talk."

Her options were slim.

Chance drew more blood and said he'd have to send it out to be analyzed to see if her ovaries were still producing eggs. If they were, he advised that they harvest as many as possible for future in vitro procedures because, according to the files, they'd used up the rest of her harvested eggs in the last procedure. There was still plenty of Jamison's frozen sperm—and more where that came from—but for a future procedure to be possible, they'd need more from her.

If not, their best chance at a family was adoption.

The thought made her feel queasy. Not so much the thought of giving someone else's child a home as much as the implications that it meant she would be barren.

Either way, Chance promised to put a rush on the lab and set an appointment for her at nine o'clock in the morning on December 31.

New Years Eve.

On the last night of the year she would learn her fate. The last night. Her last chance.

Olivia left Chance's office with a heavy heart, but a firm resolve to think positive. Chance had told her to discuss the options with Jamison—as if that was going to happen—at least not in the near future, and that made things all the worse.

As she started to tear up again, she reminded herself firmly that it wasn't over until it was over. Right now, she just had to believe the best would happen.

She didn't want to see anyone as she was leaving. When she left Chance's office, she'd mustered every ounce of calm self-control she possessed so that he wouldn't commit her to the psych ward or make her go to the Coach House Diner. Not that there was anything wrong with the diner. She'd been there on several occasions, but today it was the last place she wanted to be. Rather than sobbing her heart out in public, she wanted to be in her own house, surrounded by familiarity and the things she loved. Maybe she'd bake some bread today. She could take it to the Children's Home tomorrow. She was on the board of directors and was due for a visit.

Her shoes echoed loudly on the cold, barren hallway floors of the institute, and there was no hiding when she rounded the corner and came face-to-face with her brother Derek.

"Olivia? What are you doing here?" Derek was Paul's twin, but the two couldn't be more different if they came from different mothers. Where Paul was warm and personable, Derek was steely and calculating.

Olivia's shaking hand fluttered to her face and she swiped at her eyes. She must look a mess.

She opened her mouth to answer him, but instead, she choked on a sob.

"Livie, what's wrong?" Derek demanded. The change in him was instant. One second he was the cold professional sporting his "work face," the next he was big brother to the rescue. When he switched into that mode, Olivia automatically regressed into the role of little sister.

The next thing she new, Derek had whisked her down the hall and into his office. Behind closed doors, she found herself blubbering and confiding in him, sister to brother, divulging the bleak prognosis Chance had just leveled and confessing her marital woes.

Even though she wasn't particularly close to Derek, he always managed to get her to open up whether she wanted to or not. He had a way of getting her to confess things she didn't even share with her closest friends. Maybe it was because they were a bit removed from each other, therefore there was no risk of disappointing him or being judged.

"Jamison doesn't even know I'm here today."

Derek regarded her with a frown from across the desk, his eagle eyes sharp and piercing.

"Don't be so hard on yourself, Liv. Based on what you've told me, his not knowing might be the best thing. He wants you to wait to get pregnant, but obviously waiting might not be an option and if he won't even discuss it…well, that gives you free rein to take matters into your own hands. Who is he to dictate what you can and can't do with your body?"

Olivia felt sheepish. "Well, he is my husband."

Derek slapped the desk. "I know that, but he doesn't own you. If you want a kid, then you should have a kid. Especially you. If we were talking about Lisa, I'd be singing another tune, but you were born to be a mother."

Heat spread across Olivia's face and she felt every bit the old-fashioned, 1950s housewife. Their sister, Lisa, ran with the big boys. Even though she was the baby of the family, she had no trouble matching her brothers move for move.

"I mean if Demetrios is right—and I'd stake my own reputation on him—then you have no time to waste."

Olivia chewed on her French manicured index fingernail, hoping to stave off another wave of tears before she could speak. Once she'd composed herself, she said, "Going on what Dr. Demetrios said, if we're not able to harvest my eggs, this is all a moot point. So please don't hold it against Jamison, Derek."

Derek frowned. "I thought we'd stored your eggs?"

Olivia shook her head. "We used them up in the last in vitro attempt."

Derek squinted at her, a look that concerned her because when he pulled that expression he'd usually latched on to an idea that wasn't always conventional. Then he turned to his computer and started tap-tapping on the keys.

"What are you doing?"

He didn't answer her, but instead donned a pair of reading glasses and focused intently on his computer screen. A moment later, he said, "I've pulled up your file. I see we still have plenty of Jamison's tadpoles frozen away. Reports indicate that they're healthy and viable."

Olivia shifted in her seat. "Yes, but they're no good if I can't bring my half to the table."

"Not necessarily."

Derek pursed his lips and pinned her with his intense gaze. He had his work face on again and was firmly back in professional mode. But she recognized something else in his expression.

Olivia knew from experience that her brother's line between right and unethical was sometimes a little blurred. She had a feeling that what he was about to say next might be a little speculative.

Even so, she heard herself asking, "What do you mean?"

Derek didn't answer immediately. He paused as if giving her a chance to retract her question and get away. But she sat there as if bolted to the seat.

Derek folded his hands and rested them on his desk. Then he leaned in.

"How would you feel about using donor eggs?"

Olivia cocked her head to the side, "I couldn't do that."

Derek moistened his lips. His eyes darted from side to side. Then he pinned her with his steely gaze.

"Why not? Demetrios could fertilize a donor egg

with Jamison's sperm and the zygote could be implanted in you to carry it to term. Voilà! You'd have your baby. Problem solved."

Olivia pulled back as if her brother had offered her poison.

"Derek, it wouldn't be *my* baby."

"Olivia—" his tone mocked her "—no one outside this room has to know."

"Chance Demetrios would know. Do you remember me telling you that we were just talking about how my biological cupboard is bare?"

Derek rolled his eyes.

"Wonder boy doesn't know *everything* that goes on around this place. You have no idea the secrets we keep in here. There's a whole section of classified files to which only a select few have access."

His maniacal expression made her uncomfortable, and for a moment she wondered if he'd gone a little mad.

"If I tell Demetrios we have a special *emergency* stash of your eggs, he'll believe me."

Olivia was chewing on her fingernail again. "But why would you have a special emergency stash of my eggs? It doesn't make sense."

He looked at her as if she was insufferably dense. "Because, Olivia, you are likely going to be the first lady of our country, and that makes you pretty special. And if, perchance, there was an emergency—such as the one you find yourself in today—the eggs would be available to you. Understand?"

No, she didn't understand, because what he was suggesting sounded reprehensible. She looked at him as if in his face she could find the piece of the puzzle she was obviously missing—something to help her understand how this devious scheme could be okay.

"You're suggesting that I not include Jamison in this decision?"

Derek shrugged a single shoulder, as if he were too annoyed to expend the energy to raise and lower both.

"Go ahead and tell him if you think he'll go for it."

Of course Jamison would never go along with this plan. She felt dishonest enough even being here behind her husband's back. But even talking about getting impregnated with a child that wouldn't be fully, biologically, theirs and trying to pass it off as theirs… This…if she did *this*…well, she wouldn't be able to look her husband in the eye, much less live with herself.

She was just about ready to say *Thanks, but no thanks* when Derek said, "Livie, don't look at me like I'm a monster. The only reason I'm suggesting this is because you desperately want a child and it could very well save your troubled marriage."

His words hit like a painful punch to the gut.

"I know it's a lot to think about, but keep an open mind. I'm going to go ahead and relabel the eggs—they're all from the same woman and according to the file she even has your coloring—just in case your New Year's Eve test results don't come back the way you'd hoped."

As much as she hated to admit it, Derek had a point. What if the test results proved that she'd waited too long? What if using donor eggs was her only option?

Jamison would never agree to it.

But she'd already come this far.

What if what Jamison didn't know was the only thing that could save their marriage?

She certainly had a lot to think about before she dismissed this final option.

Chapter Six

Before heading off to dinner, Jamison excused himself from the delegation of Middle Eastern dignitaries and ducked inside his office to call Olivia.

After living apart for more than two months then seeing her for two days, he didn't think he could go four more days without her.

He missed her that much.

So when the group started making noises about staying in D.C. through the New Year, Jamison had promptly told them he'd be happy to leave them in the capable hands of his aide, Cameron McInerney, but he wouldn't be in town.

The dignitaries protested but Jamison simply joked that if he left his wife at home alone on New Year's Eve he'd have to spend the rest of the year making it up to her.

When the visiting sheikh shared his philosophy that women should never dictate a man's actions—especially when it interfered with business—Jamison retorted respectfully, "Obviously, you've never met my wife."

And he meant it as a sincere compliment.

It wasn't that Jamison was heading home out of obligation. Not this time. As he'd said goodbye to Olivia earlier in the week, something had shifted. Right now, he longed to see his wife. He longed to wipe the slate clean. Longed to start off the New Year right.

With Olivia in his arms.

Somewhere recently he'd heard the idiom "a happy wife makes for a happy life." It made so much sense. If she was happy, he wouldn't have to worry about her seeking comfort in another man's arms. With Olivia as his top priority all his plans would fall into place: his congressional work, his eventual bid for the White House (because what would it mean without Olivia by his side?) and their family.

He'd been thinking and, depending on how things were between them this next week, maybe they should start trying again.

That's why he needed to call her right now.

She answered on the second ring.

"Hello?"

"Hi, Liv, it's me."

She paused a few beats too long.

"Jamison. Is everything okay?"

"Yes. Everything's fine. I was thinking about you and wanted to call."

"Oh, I see. That's very sweet."

She sounded a little distant and formal. He wanted so badly to pull her into his arms and show her that everything was going to be okay.

"I'm also calling for another reason," he said.

"What?" She sounded wary. "You're not calling to tell me you can't make it home for New Year's Eve, are you?"

"Don't worry," he said, eager to put her mind at rest. "Actually, I'm calling to find out what your plans are on New Year's Eve."

She was silent on the other end of the line, and for a moment, he wondered if they'd lost their telephone connection.

"Olivia, are you there?"

"Yes. I'm here." She still sounded guarded and distant. "What do you mean?"

He sat down behind his desk and picked up a photo of her. The juxtaposition of seeing her beautiful face smiling at him from the frame and hearing her sound so remote on the line made his heart ache.

"I'm calling to ask you out on a date. This is my feeble attempt at being romantic." He chuckled, then his voice got serious. "After being apart for so long, I didn't want to be presumptuous and assume you'd be waiting for me."

"Thank you, Jamison. But of course, I wouldn't make plans without you."

Her saying that made him smile.

"I'll be home late afternoon and we can do whatever you want. We can go out and paint the town or we can order in and have a nice quiet evening alone together." He hesitated. "Maybe we could spend the whole night in bed and start talking about…babies?"

"Oh, Jamison." Her voice caught on his name. "As long as we're together. That's all that matters."

He let out a breath of relief. Now that the world had finally righted itself again, it almost felt as if it could start spinning in the right direction.

"Even though Christmas didn't go as planned, seeing you again after being apart for so long made me realize how much I love you. It also made me realize that even though I couldn't admit it to myself until now, I've been afraid to start our family. Growing up in a broken home—knowing how my father's leaving affected my mother and brothers, seeing what the hormones did to you, what the experience did to us, I guess I wasn't as prepared as I thought I was. But knowing how important having a baby is to you... Let's just not let it change *us,* okay?"

Olivia held the phone for a moment, although their call had ended, using it as a touchstone. In the span of mere seconds, she'd gone from being petrified that Jamison was calling to cancel their plans yet again to through-the-ceiling joy after hearing Jamison say he was ready to start trying for a baby again. That bipolar moment had finally evened out, settling somewhere in the middle, tempered by the guilty secret she was keeping from her husband. The only way she could fix this was to tell him that she'd already started seeing the doctor again without him.

But she couldn't tell him just yet.

Not when he'd just come around. After fearing a baby would change their relationship, he'd need more time for the baby idea to gel before she told him the truth—that she'd moved forward without him.

Not to mention that, first, she needed to hear her final prognosis.

The next day, Jamison didn't pick up the call from Cameron. He let it go to voice mail along with the other two-dozen voice mails McInerney had left that day. It was their routine, of sorts. Anything that could wait went to voice mail to be checked at designated times during the day. But when something needed urgent attention, Cameron followed up with a 911 text.

The 911 came in at 2:22, the afternoon after he'd talked to Olivia to make plans for New Year's Eve. The text read: Have received the background check on Dr. Chance Demetrios. Results require your immediate attention.

Chance Demetrios?

He'd been so busy, he'd put Demetrios out of his mind. Besides, it was just a momentary lapse of reasoning. He trusted his wife. So the message sent a jolt of anxiety through him. Jamison excused himself from the meeting, citing urgent business.

What McInerney had waiting for him when he got back to the office made the anxiety he'd felt earlier seem like a warm bath: photos shot outside the Armstrong Institute. Photos of Olivia in the arms of Chance Demetrios.

Jamison wanted to punch a wall. He wanted to hop on a plane and punch Demetrios. He wanted to look his wife in the eyes and ask, *"Why?"*

He would ask her, all right. When he saw her in three days. In the meantime, though, he couldn't talk to her. He needed to keep his distance, keep his cool, so that he didn't do something he'd regret. Also, if he heard her voice there would be no way he'd be able to keep this to himself. And he needed to see her eyes when he asked her about it.

How the hell was he going to hold this inside for three days?

He ran through the options in his mind. He could cancel his meetings, saying he had a family emergency to attend to.

No, if in fact Olivia was carrying on with Demetrios…though his heart still couldn't reconcile her betraying him like that—not his Olivia. No, if he left it might draw attention to the situation, and he had to do everything he could to keep this under wraps.

As anger simmered, he felt like a ticking time bomb that he hoped wouldn't explode before he gave Olivia a chance to explain.

Chapter Seven

Dressed in a cobalt-blue suit and pearls, Olivia drove across the Salt-and-Pepper Bridge, which stretched over the Charles River, connecting Boston with Cambridge.

The formal name of the bridge was actually the Longfellow, but locals had dubbed it "Salt-and-Pepper" because the structure's central towers resembled salt-and-pepper shakers.

The Children's Home was located just across the river, not too far from the Massachusetts Institute of Technology. Olivia had served on the Children's Home board since the year she and Jamison had

married. Before she'd been appointed to the
Children's Home board of directors, she'd volun-
teered there when she was in college and knew it was
such a worthy organization that it deserved as much
support as it could get.

In the nearly ten years that she'd been involved,
Olivia had been instrumental in helping Pam Wilson,
the executive director of The Children's Home, write
grants, raise funds and secure other means of political and community support for the Home.

Other times, she filled in where they needed her.
Whether it was answering the phone, taking the kids
shopping for school supplies, or rolling up her
sleeves and scrubbing toilets when the janitorial
service didn't show, she did what she could. Her
favorite task was baking dozens of delicious cookies
for the kids to take to school for birthday celebrations
or bake sales, or sometimes the cookies were simply
for them to enjoy as a special treat.

Olivia's goal as president of the board was to give
the children—many of whom were here because of
abuse, neglect or tragedy—as good a childhood as
possible. Sometimes that meant singing songs and
reading stories. Other times it meant getting her
hands dirty. But she was game for whatever the kids
needed, because she was passionate about the
Children's Home and the kids they served.

It was never easy, though, when a new resident arrived. Usually the child was scared and skittish, oftentimes suffering emotional trauma after being displaced. Today, Pam needed all hands on deck because not one, but two little boys were arriving.

Danny and Kevin Kelso had lost both of their parents in a nightmarish accident on the day after Christmas. The parents were coming home from a party and were hit head-on by a drunk driver. The boys had been home asleep in their beds, in the care of a babysitter.

Since the boys had no living relatives, Boston's Department of Children and Families had prevailed upon Pam to take the boys so that they could stay together. The home really didn't have room, but when Pam called Olivia for special dispensation, Olivia had agreed that the boys should stay together at all costs—even if she had to bring them to her house until the Home could make a place for them.

Keeping them together seemed extra important since three-year-old Danny had recently been diagnosed with autism.

Little had she known when she'd decided to distract herself with baking bread and cookies, that the home would be in need of fare to welcome the new charges.

There was nothing like good, homemade sugar and

chocolate chunk cookies to make a child feel welcome.

Olivia had promised Pam that she'd be there to help, because even under the best circumstances, welcoming a new resident wasn't easy. Given the younger Kelso boy's situation, today was sure to be doubly challenging.

Shortly after nine o'clock, Olivia arrived at the Georgian-style mansion that housed the Children's Home. The old home once belonged to the charity's founder, who left it to the organization in trust to be used for kids left homeless or orphaned by abuse, neglect or tragedy. Olivia parked around back by the carriage house, which served as the nonprofit's offices, and let herself in the kitchen door. She set the bread and cookies on the counter and went in search of Pam, whom she found in the great room.

"Olivia, thank you so much for coming in today," Pam said. "It seems like a lot to ask during the holidays."

Olivia shook her head. "I'm happy to do it. Besides, Jamison had to go back to D.C. and he won't be back until New Year's Eve."

"Big plans?" Pam asked.

Olivia blushed. "We're staying in and having a nice romantic evening—alone, for a change."

Over the years, Pam had become a friend—and

someone to whom in the beginning, Olivia had confided in when she and Jamison had decided to start trying to get pregnant. But after it became clear that pregnancy wouldn't come easily—and then with the ensuing bumps in their marriage—Olivia had become a bit more guarded.

"Really?" Pam arched a brow, her blue eyes shining. "Anything you'd care to share?"

For a moment, Olivia was tempted to tell her everything—well, almost everything—not about Derek's bizarre suggestion that Olivia try to pass off another woman's child as her own. Because essentially that's what it would amount to if she allowed Chance to implant another woman's egg in her body.

The thought made her shudder, and that brought her to her senses. Despite how good it would feel to confide in a friend right now, until she heard the New Year's Eve prognosis, she needed to keep everything to herself.

"Oh, nothing exciting, but you know I'll tell you as soon as there's news."

Just then the door opened and two of the saddest little boys Olivia had ever seen walked in hand in hand. Both had mops of glossy dark hair and large, haunted brown eyes.

The larger of the two stood slightly in front of his younger brother, in a protective stance.

Karen Cunningham from DCF stood behind them. "Good morning, I have a very special delivery for you. This is Kevin." She gestured to the older brother. "And this little guy is Danny."

"Hello, boys. I'm Pam, and this is Mrs. Mallory. We want you to know you are very welcome here."

The boys gaped at her but remained silent.

"You make yourselves right at home," Pam said. "Mrs. Mallory is here for you while Mrs. Cunningham and I go take care of some paperwork."

Olivia knelt in front of the boys.

"Hi, guys. Now, tell me again, which one of you is Kevin and which one is Danny?"

"I'm Kevin," said the older brother. "I'm seven years old."

Olivia offered her hand to the boy. "Hi, Kevin. You can call me Olivia, if you'd like."

Kevin shook her hand like a little man, much too grown up for his age.

"He's Danny, he doesn't talk because he's special."

"Hi, Danny." She offered her hand to the smaller boy just as she'd done for the older brother, but he didn't take it. Instead, he started rocking back and forth, paying no attention to Olivia.

"He's sad because our mommy and daddy got killed in a real bad car wreck."

Kevin's lower lip quivered and for a moment Olivia

thought he might cry. She was surprised when he didn't.

She took his hand in hers again. "Kevin, it's okay to cry. I know you must be very sad, too. Just like Danny is."

Still holding Olivia's hand, Kevin focused on a spot somewhere over her shoulder and didn't let down his guard.

Olivia squeezed his hand. "Well, I want you to know I think you're very brave, but even the bravest men in the world cry sometimes. And that's okay."

Suddenly, Danny stepped forward, reached and touched Olivia's pearl necklace.

"Duck!" said Danny.

Kevin grabbed his brother's hand and held it.

"Don't touch, Danny."

"Duck!" Danny repeated.

Olivia gazed down into his little upturned face and smiled. She pointed at her necklace. "These are pearls, Danny."

Kevin shook his head. "It doesn't matter how many times you tell him. He's still going to call it a duck, because that's what he thinks it is. I told you, he's *special* and he doesn't know any better."

Olivia nodded and gave Kevin a conspiratorial wink. "That's good to know. If he wants to call it a duck, then this can be my…duck. Say, Kevin, do you and Danny like cookies? I just made some. They're in the kitchen. Why don't we go get some?"

Kevin's face shuttered again.

"My mommy doesn't let us eat cookies between meals."

His little bottom lip trembled again, but he raised his chin a notch and refocused on his spot over Olivia's shoulder.

Her heart was breaking for these two sweet boys. She was about to tell Kevin that she was sure his mother wouldn't mind just this once, and praise him for following her rules, when Danny's hand snaked out again and grabbed a hold of Olivia's necklace.

"Duck!" he yelled, and gave them a firm yank.

His grasp was far stronger than she might have imagined because the necklace broke. If not for the individual knots between each pearl, the necklace might have scattered all over the floor. Instead, the broken strand held together in a limp line trailing down Danny's arm.

"Danny! No!" reprimanded Kevin.

He turned to Olivia. "I'm sorry. I'm really, really sorry. Please don't be mad at him. Please—"

With that, his voice broke and he dissolved into a heap of full-body sobs.

Reflexively, Olivia gathered him in her arms and held him while he cried on the shoulder of her blue suit.

Rubbing his back, she said, "I'm not mad. It was just a silly old duck anyway. I can get it fixed later."

Pam and Karen rushed in to see what all the commotion was about, but Olivia waved them away. She was no expert, but instincts told her that now that Kevin was finally letting down his guard, now that he was finally allowing himself to feel his loss, the last thing he needed was an audience gawking at him.

As he continued to sob on her shoulder, she mouthed to them, *It's okay. He'll be fine.* Hesitant, they retreated to Pam's office, throwing concerned glances Olivia's way as she rubbed the boy's back in slow, circular motions.

Of all people, she understood the loss he was grappling with—only in reverse. She'd had a hard time processing the sense of loss she felt, not being able to get pregnant. The loss—or empty spot—in her life that Jamison's and her child was supposed to occupy. It felt like a gaping hole in the place where her heart beat. Some days she wanted to sob on someone's shoulder, too, but instead, like Kevin, she'd chosen the stoic path.

She pulled the weeping boy closer. Holding him, for the first time ever, she felt that gaping hole begin to close.

"Duck?" Danny murmured.

"Duck," she whispered, smiling at him through her own unshed tears.

Once the boys were settled in the dining room at the table enjoying milk and cookies with the other Children's Home residents, Olivia and Pam retreated into Pam's office.

Pam slid in behind her desk and Olivia claimed the chair facing it.

"Here's the report from Danny's doctor." She nudged a slim stack of papers across her desk toward Olivia. "Karen filled me in on Danny's condition. Apparently, he was recently diagnosed with Autism Spectrum Disorder, and he had just started speech and behavior therapy before the holidays."

Olivia skimmed the report. "So, he's not enrolled in school yet?"

Pam shook her head. "He just turned three in November and I believe they were waiting until after the first of the year to enroll him in a public school exceptional educational program. But with all that's happened, we're going to have to talk to his doctor and see what he suggests is the best course of action. The little guy has had so much to digest, losing his parents and all, that I'm not certain starting him in a new program right away will be the best thing."

The fifteen other kids who lived at the Children's Home were all in school. That meant Danny would need someone to look after him during the day. Pam would have to bring in one of the part-time employees to help out. It would further tax the organization's already stretched budget.

"I can come in a couple of days a week to help out," Olivia offered. She wished she could offer more—for one quick, insane moment, she was about ready to offer for Danny and Kevin to come live with her. But it was an irrational thought. Completely emotional and off the cuff. With her steady lineup of doctor's appointments, she'd be lucky to be able to give Pam two solid days of help per week.

Her heart was breaking for the boys. She wanted to ease their grief and give them…a home. But what would happen once her baby arrived? Reflexively, she slid a hand over her stomach.

She couldn't adopt them. No, it was best to let the boys get settled into their new home. That was the right thing to do.

Even so, why did leaving them here feel completely wrong?

Chapter Eight

Three days later, Olivia awoke early and placed yet another call to Jamison. It was New Year's Eve and she'd been trying to reach him for the past two days. All the calls went to voice mail, and he had yet to return a single call.

As she'd done at least a dozen times already, she left yet another message.

"Jamison, it's *me*. I don't understand why you're not calling me back. I'm worried."

What she didn't say, despite the urge, was that it was six o'clock in the morning and she couldn't reach him at home, the office or on his cell.

What was with this sudden change in him? Just a few days ago, everything seemed so good. Now here she was, wondering not only if her husband was letting business preempt their plans, but also if maybe he was going to stand her up altogether.

No. He wouldn't do that. Would he?

In the months that they'd been separated, he'd never gone more than a day without calling her. And he'd certainly never let her calls go unanswered. She didn't understand the sudden change in him, which sent her into another spiral of panic that maybe something was wrong.

She had no choice but to call McInerney to make sure Jamison was okay. She got his voice mail, too.

"Cameron, hello, this is Olivia. I'm trying to reach my husband. When you talk to him, will you please ask him to call me? Thank you."

She hung up the phone in disbelief. All the worry and anxiety on top of this being the day that Dr. Demetrios would have her test results.

Nervous, she brewed herself a cup of cinnamon apple tea and took the delicate china cup upstairs to the window seat in the master bedroom.

The cold December air seeped in through the windowpanes. From her perch on the third floor, she could see across Commonwealth Avenue, over the tops of the stately trees that lined the street where she lived, straight into Public Garden. The garden and adjacent Boston Common were an oasis in the heart of densely populated downtown Boston. A sanctuary laced with gorgeous statues, it was a haven even in the dead of winter.

Olivia pressed her hand to the glass and the cold bit her palm, as if it were taunting her. When she and Jamison had purchased the house, proximity to the lovely park was one of the things that completed their dream house. Since the day they'd moved in, Olivia had fantasized about arranging long playdates at the park for their children, and spending leisurely Sunday afternoons on a picnic blanket while Jamison tossed the football with their kids.

The ringing phone startled her from her reverie and she spilled hot tea on herself as she stumbled for the phone.

Finally, she thought as she grabbed up the receiver.

"Jamison?"

There was a long pause on the other end of the line before a male voice—not Jamison's—said, "Good morning, Mrs. Mallory. This is Cameron McInerney. I hope I'm not calling too early, but I see on my call log that you called a few moments ago."

"Yes, I did. Is Jamison okay?"

Another pause. "Yes, ma'am, he's fine. In fact, he

asked me to call you and let you know that his flight gets in at six this afternoon. He will be home shortly thereafter."

Confused as to why Cameron was calling her rather than her husband taking the time to do so, Olivia paced as she listened.

"Cameron, I appreciate your call, but why isn't Jamison calling me himself? I have been leaving messages for days."

Again, Cameron paused a few beats too long. Finally, he said, "I don't know, ma'am. I'm simply relaying the message he asked me to deliver."

When they hung up, a chill seemed to permeate the air. Something wasn't right. Despite how she tried to blame her uneasiness on nerves over her appointment with Dr. Demetrios, Olivia knew she was justified being upset with Jamison.

Couldn't he even spare five minutes to call her himself?

At least he still planned to be home this evening, and she had a doctor's appointment to get ready for. Right now she needed to use every ounce of energy to prepare herself for the news Chance Demetrios had waiting for her.

News that was going to change her life...one way or another.

* * *

Olivia paused in the threshold of Paul's office and knocked lightly on the door frame. Her brother scowled up at her from the open magazine on his desk, *Northeastern Journal of Medicine*. When he saw her, he closed the magazine and changed his expression in a flash.

"Well, hello! Look who it is." His voice rang with cheer, and if she hadn't seen the annoyance on his face a moment ago, she might have believed nothing was wrong.

"I'm a little early for my follow-up with Chance, and I thought I'd stop by and say hi," she said. "I don't mean to disturb you."

He drummed his fingers on his desk.

"Of course you're not disturbing me. Come in. Please." He gestured toward the chair in front of his desk.

"What are you reading?" she asked.

"Nothing."

"It sure looked like something judging by the way you were scowling. Is everything okay?"

He breathed an exasperated sigh and raked a hand through his curly, dark hair. In that moment of letdown, she could see the dark circles under his brown eyes. He looked exhausted.

Olivia reached out across the desk and touched his arm. "What is it, Paul?"

He shook his head. "I might as well tell you now, because it's likely to come out in the near future."

Paul hesitated and held up the issue of the medical journal he'd been reading when she walked in.

"The institute is teetering on the brink of a public relations disaster. It's a nightmare, Liv. A ticking time bomb that could explode in our faces if we don't act fast and smart."

She'd never seen her brother look so distressed, not in all the years since he'd picked up the Armstrong reins and started running the fertility institute that his father had dedicated his life to building.

"What's going on?"

Paul cleared his throat. "This periodical ran a story saying that the institute used donor eggs and sperm to impregnate many wealthy couples."

"Right, there's nothing wrong with that. That's what you do here."

Paul frowned. "They alleged that some of the couples were unaware of the substitutions. That they thought they were impregnated with their own sperm and eggs."

A cold wave of shock slapped her, and Olivia's blood turned to ice. That sounded exactly like what Derek had suggested she do. Except he'd told her. He hadn't tried to do the substitution behind her back. Though he'd urged her to lie to her husband in exactly that same way.

Oh, my God. "Paul, forgive me, but I have to ask. Is the allegation true?"

Her brother pulled a face. "Of course it's not true. I can't believe you'd think for even one second that it would be."

She felt queasy watching her brother in such distress. His identity was so closely tied to the institute that if one questioned the business practices, they were essentially questioning his personal integrity.

Paul took pride in his scrupulously clean record. Derek, however, was altogether another animal. It was amazing how twin brothers could be such polar opposites.

Slow simmering anger roiled in the pit of her stomach as Derek's suggestion rang her ears. There was no way she could tell Paul that Derek had essentially offered her the same arrangement.

No, if she told him, World War Three would erupt.

Even so, the longer she thought about it, the more she wondered if there was, perhaps, some truth to the allegation…brought on by Derek's doings.

Somehow, she managed to ask, "What are you going to do about it?"

Paul sighed. "It's tricky. Right now, only two

minor medical journals have run the story. None of
the mainstream news outlets have picked up on it—
yet. Our attorneys have threatened to slap the pub-
lishers with libel suits, because they presented no
hard proof."

But *she* had proof. *Right from Derek's mouth.*

"The problem is," he continued, "if we file, it's
likely to let the cat out of the bag. Reporters are
always trolling the court dockets. They could easily
get wind of the case that way."

Olivia scooted forward in her seat. "They're going
to print a retraction, aren't they? They have to, since
they have no proof."

Uncertainty clouded his expression. "That's
another dangerous catch twenty-two. On one hand,
it would be vindicating to have them admit in the
pages of their own journals they were wrong.
However, they'd probably bury the retractions in a
places where they would go unnoticed. Besides, re-
hashing only gives new life to the story. Every day
that the story goes unnoticed by the mass media
means there's less of a possibility that it'll be discovered and broadcast to the world. So, a retraction
could do more harm than good in the long run."

Olivia's mind swirled with doubt over whether
she was doing the right thing by keeping the secret
from Paul. But no, no, she had to talk to Derek

first. As she stood to go, she asked, "So, you're not going to do anything except hope it'll die a quick, silent death?"

Paul nodded.

"Unless the story explodes in the mass media. Heaven forbid, but if that happens we'll slap libel suits on both journals faster than they can say shoddy reporting. In the meantime, we're putting together a crisis PR plan that we hope we won't have to use."

"I'm with you on that," she said as she edged toward the door. "I hope you don't have to use it. Listen, I'm sorry this has happened. Please keep me posted, okay? But I have to go."

Olivia glanced at her watch as she made her way through the institute's empty halls. She had ten minutes until her appointment. Just enough time to have a chat with Derek.

So the institute had come under fire for egg swapping? And Paul was claiming it wasn't true?

Paul, she knew, was as ethical and squeaky clean as they came. She couldn't say that much for her other brother, though. If he smelled money or a way to feather the nest, the ethics line blurred.

Had he gone too far this time? From what Paul said it sounded as if this could set the institute up for a legal mess. It wouldn't only tarnish the family name, it would destroy her father's life's work.

A thought struck her and she stopped in her tracks.

The scandal might even be big enough to affect Jamison's career. Because in politics, every skeleton and scandal was fair game and fodder for mudslinging.

A scandal of this magnitude could seriously set back Jamison's shot for the presidency. The realization nearly knocked the wind out of Olivia.

Strike one: Jamison's mother had never been very fond of Olivia.

Strike two: Olivia hadn't been able to give him children.

Even if he didn't want them now, he would eventually. That's what the Mallory family was all about. They were one big, boisterous, the-more-the-merrier kind of clan, and once Jamison worked through these fears, he'd realize the importance of a family.

If, heaven forbid, there was a strike three—an Armstrong family scandal—it could spell the end of their marriage.

She flung open Derek's office door, walked in and closed it behind her.

He glanced up from his computer, peering at her over the top of his reading glasses, looking plenty annoyed.

"Well, come in, Olivia." His voice was dark with indignity. "Make yourself right at home."

She walked toward him.

"Have you been switching donor sperm and eggs, Derek?" Her voice held all the fury that had been bottling up over the months that she and Jamison had been apart.

Derek reared back in his chair, looking utterly confused. "Excuse me?"

She leaned in over his desk. "You heard me. Have you been switching donor sperm and eggs to keep wealthy clients at the institute?"

He blew out a breath between his pursed lips. "Are you talking about that ridiculous story that ran in that hack medical journal?"

He laughed, and something about the hollow sound convinced Olivia he was covering up something.

"I'm talking about the story that ran in those journals. A story with allegations alarmingly similar to the solution you offered me the last time I was here."

He smirked. "Oh, don't be ridiculous. There's no similarities there whatsoever. Who told you about this, anyway?"

"Paul told me," Olivia spat. "And he's pretty upset over it. Have you been engaging in unethical practices? This could ruin the institute, Derek!"

"Olivia, I simply offered you a means of saving your troubled marriage. That's all. There are no similarities between what that rag asserted and what I offered you. If I'd done what the journal suggested, then I wouldn't have told you. I would've just relabeled the viable eggs with your name. Good grief, Olivia. What kind of monster do you take me for?"

She hated it when he talked down to her. But she wouldn't let him intimidate her.

"Would you please explain where the eggs you offered me came from? Whose eggs are they?"

He looked at her as if she had two heads. As if this was painfully simple and she should understand. "They're donor eggs. Ovum we paid for so we could help women like you who can't produce eggs of their own. Pardon me for trying to help you."

His words were a low blow even if they were true. He must've seen it in her face because he softened his tone.

"The ones I offered you are from our 'egg bank' and are absolutely free and clear. They do not 'belong' to anyone but the future recipient."

He regarded her for a moment with piercing brown eyes. The longer he stared at her, the smaller Olivia felt.

"I'm sorry," she whispered. "I didn't mean to accuse you of anything. But I still don't understand why you implied there should be so much secrecy around giving me the eggs? Changing the files so that everyone thought they were mine rather than donor eggs? I mean, Derek, come on, you have to admit the allegations in the exposé mirror your offer."

Derek sighed and rolled his eyes.

"There is no similarity whatsoever. The secrecy was simply for your and Jamison's benefit—for privacy. As I said, I was just offering you a way to save your marriage and a means of keeping up appearances. Now, if you don't mind, I have to get back to work."

He got up, walked to the door and opened it.

Olivia exited his office. When the door clicked behind her, she was in greater turmoil than when she'd entered.

She dialed Jamison's cell, but got his voice mail. *Again.*

She was tired of pretending their marriage was solid. Would having a baby actually save their troubled relationship? For the first time ever, she wasn't so sure.

She heard footsteps down at the end of the hall and looked up. It was Chance Demetrios. The man with the results. The answer that was key to the rest of her life.

"There you are." His voice was maddeningly neutral. Neither happy nor sad. "I got your test results back. Why don't we go to my office and discuss them."

They walked in silence. Olivia was glad he didn't try to make conversation, because she was still suffering aftershock from the conversation with her brothers.

"I have news," he said. "And I have *better* news. Where would you like me to start?"

Olivia sighed. "Give me the *better* news first. I think I need to start in a good place."

When Chance nodded, Olivia noticed that he looked solemn. Her gut clenched and she laced her hands protectively over her belly.

"When I was reviewing your file, I saw something I'd overlooked. Apparently, the doctor you saw before I arrived at the Armstrong Institute harvested and flash-froze a couple of emergency stashes of your eggs."

Olivia tensed. So Derek had gone through with the egg transfer after all, even though he hadn't mentioned it earlier. She hadn't really given him a chance to get a word in.

"I'm guessing that despite his not indicating it in your file, the doctor must have suspected there was a problem with egg production since he had the foresight to freeze thirty eggs. That gives us enough for three more in vitro procedures."

Three more.

Suddenly, with a breath-stealing blow, it dawned on her where this conversation was going.

"What's the other news you mentioned?"

She braced herself, knowing what he was going to say and feeling queasy because of it.

"I'm sorry, Olivia. Your tests prove that your ovaries

have stopped producing eggs. I hate to be so blunt, but if you want to have a baby, I suggest that we start the procedure as soon as possible since you'll need to be on the hormones for about three weeks before we can fertilize your eggs and implant the embryos. Would you like to start the hormones today?"

Tongue-tied and shaken, she stared at him. She hadn't been prepared to act this quickly since she thought they'd simply be discussing the test results.

"So, you're saying I don't have any time to waste?"

Dr. Demetrios rubbed his chin with one hand as he regarded her.

"I suggest you not let too much time pass. But if you need to think about it, or perhaps discuss it with your husband, we can start the hormones on your next visit. It's up to you."

Why was she hesitating?

Why was she so conflicted?

The need to have a child had driven her here today—without her husband. Was it her conscience, or simply self-doubt making her waver? She wanted a baby more than anything. Yet a little voice deep inside her was whispering that if she walked out that door without setting the process in motion today, it might be hard to come back.

Dr. Demetrios smiled at her. "What would you like to do, Olivia?"

Chapter Nine

Jamison used the flight to Boston's Logan Airport and the subsequent ride home to mentally prepare himself for seeing Olivia.

He'd had the days since seeing the photos to weigh all the options, to look at the situation from all angles and to think about what he would do when he saw her.

It had opened up childhood wounds he'd thought had healed over the years, brought back memories of his distraught mother crying over the telephone, desperately trying to track down her husband. In those days of no cell phones or pagers, when a person wanted to get lost, it was a lot easier than it was today.

Judson Mallory would sometimes *get lost* for days. His staff would cover for him, inventing meetings that Helen had no way of confirming or disproving.

Of course, Jamison had been too young to know what was really going on when his father would disappear. All he knew is that there would be long stretches of absence during which the household staff would care for him and his brothers because his mother "had taken ill."

As Jamison got older, it didn't take long to realize his mother wasn't really sick at all. She was either too drunk to function or too hung over from the benders brought on by her husband's going MIA.

It wasn't until years later, long after his father had died, that once-faithful friends and confidants crawled out of the woodwork offering tell-all books detailing that all wasn't as rosy as it seemed behind the manicured Mallory hedges.

Piece by painful piece, Jamison learned about a much darker side of the man he and an adoring public had idolized. The havoc that his father's womanizing had wreaked on their family and the subsequent betrayal by friends was enough to convince Jamison that he would never live his personal life the way his father had—fathering six boys he'd never wanted and leaving all responsibility for them to a mother who was unable to cope.

Jamison did want a family…someday. But he didn't want to repeat his father's mistakes. He wanted to wait until he was ready. Obviously with the way he was waffling back and forth—one minute ready to do it because it would make his wife happy, but the next minute feeling so unsure about his marriage, which in turn made him feel uncertain about having kids—meant that he wasn't.

In the same way that he'd committed to marriage once he'd pledged his life to Olivia, he felt that strongly about waiting until his marriage was on firmer ground before having children. Especially now that there was the possibility that his wife had strayed.

On the car ride home from the airport, he thought about the photos and what might have driven Olivia into another man's arms. He knew he'd been a little selfish over the past couple of years, a little insensitive to her needs. The purely rational side of him that could separate facts and emotion—the attorney in him—had leveled the verdict that maybe this had driven her to another man. But that was about as far as the rational side went. The thought of her in another man's arms nearly drove him over the edge.

So he clung to the last shred of hope he had. That even though the photos showed Olivia in Demetrios's arms—in an embrace that looked intimate—there wasn't a single shot of them kissing…or worse.

The fact that there was no kiss left a huge gray area open to interpretation. That's when common sense dictated that he had to give Olivia the benefit of the doubt. And he still needed to see her face—her eyes—when he presented the photos. That would be key.

He knew her, and he'd be able to recognize if she was lying about something. But at least he'd had time to figure out that he was willing to fight for his marriage if Olivia was willing to meet him halfway.

Of course, they'd be back at awkward square one. Another thought that remained constant in his mind as he sorted out everything was that he was glad there were no children involved.

So, despite his earlier, impulsive change of heart, essentially they were back at the starting line. He'd have to insist that they mend their marriage before they brought a child into their world. He'd grown up in a broken home and, above all else, he'd vowed to never put a child of his own through that hell.

His father had strayed and his mother had put him out. Had Olivia been talking about having his child one minute and then turning to another man the next?

No!

He wouldn't jump to conclusions. He wouldn't trip down that slippery path, he reminded himself.

The car turned onto his street and stopped in front of his house—their house.

He'd go inside, hear Olivia out and then they'd decide together if their house was still a home.

Olivia felt bare without her pearls. They'd been a gift from Jamison and in some ways they were like a link to him when he was away. Wearing them made her feel connected to him. They made her feel safe. She'd taken them to the jeweler to be restrung as soon as she'd left the Children's Home, but because of the holidays, they wouldn't be ready until next week.

She put her hand up to her naked throat. She'd tried other necklaces, but none felt right. Even though she felt bare without them, and she wanted to look her best for Jamison, she felt better with nothing at her neck than something that was not her pearls.

Maybe she'd opt for a brooch instead. She pulled a white-gold snowflake pin out of her jewelry box and was just about ready to pin it to her emerald-green cashmere sweater when she heard the alarm signal that someone had just opened the front door.

Jamison?

Her heart raced. She was as nervous as a high school girl awaiting her first date—and not being one hundred percent sure the guy of her dreams would actually show to pick her up.

She breathed a sigh of relief that he was finally home. But that relief was soon pinched by the ugly reminder that for days Jamison hadn't even had the time or desire to call her.

She considered pretending nothing was wrong, so as not to spoil their time together. Really, the last thing she wanted was another fight. But she knew herself well enough to realize that it would be best to get it off her mind first thing, stating her case plainly and without drama rather than letting it come out explosively at a random moment.

She wasn't being a nag. She had a valid reason to be upset. First, work had preempted their holiday—and she'd been understanding. But then, he had taken her compliance for granted and decided he didn't even need to talk to her.

Enough was enough.

Her hand was shaking too badly to pin on the brooch. So she returned it to her jewelry box and headed downstairs to say her piece.

She found him sitting in the living room. He hadn't fixed himself a drink as she'd imagined he would. He was simply sitting there in the overstuffed burgundy chair with his elbows braced on the arms and his chin in his hand. A large manila envelope lay in his lap.

He didn't smile when she walked into the room. He just sat there watching her with a neutral expression.

"Well, welcome home, stranger." Her tone was a touch more sarcastic than she'd intended, but he didn't seem to notice. He just sat there with a deadpan expression that was starting to annoy her.

She walked over and sat on the edge of the chintz sofa that was closest to him. His chin didn't move from his hand, but his gaze followed her.

"Jamison, look, I don't want to fight with you, but I think we need to have a little chat and clear up a few things before we do anything else tonight."

"You're right." Jamison reached over and set the manila envelope on the coffee table in front of her.

"What's this?" she asked.

He glowered at her "Why don't you open it and tell me, Olivia?"

Olivia eyed him speculatively, wondering for a moment if she should tell him his envelope would have to wait until after she'd said what she needed to say. But curiosity got the better of her and, a moment later, she found herself holding a stack of five-by-seven photos.

She did a double take when she realized they were photos of herself—in the arms of Dr. Chance Demetrios.

"What is this?" she asked as numbness engulfed her.

"Why don't you tell me, Olivia? I think you're the one who needs to explain."

She blinked at Jamison, confused. Then as her gaze skittered from him to the photos, and back to him, an ugly realization set in.

"You had me followed? Why, Jamison? Why would you do that?"

He gestured toward the photos. "For obvious reasons that are self-explanatory."

Her heart drummed a furious cadence, and she stared at the photos again, this time taking a longer look.

"I don't understand," she said. "Tell me exactly what it is you think you see."

He scooted to the edge of his chair and braced his arms on his knees. "I see my wife in another man's arms. The very man who called my house on the morning I left for D.C."

What? Olivia squinted at him. "How do you know he called?"

His brows shot up. "I checked the caller ID when I went back into the bedroom. Chance Demetrios's number came up. Do you deny that you talked to him?"

Jamison sounded like a lawyer prosecuting his case. She hated it when he took that superior tone with her.

"Stop talking down to me." She flung the photos onto the coffee table. "I am not on trial."

Jamison flinched and his face softened to a heart-breaking look of anguish.

"No, you're not. But…" He gestured to the photos. Then, as he reached down and picked up one, Olivia saw that he had tears in his eyes.

Oh, my God. This is why he wouldn't return my calls.

"Jamison, listen to me. This is *wrong* on so many levels that I don't even know where to begin. Except to say it's not what it looks like. I am not having an affair with Chance Demetrios."

His throat worked in a hard swallow, and he looked her square in the eyes. She held his gaze. "Why don't you start at the beginning?"

The beginning? Where did the story begin? Their relationship had been deteriorating for so long, she really didn't know where to start. Even so, she knew she had to tell him the truth.

"Chance Demetrios is my doctor."

Jamison nodded. "I'm aware of that. Until the photos, I was aware that you'd seen him once a few months ago. For professional reasons."

"He called the morning you left because I told Paul I'd like to schedule another appointment with him."

Jamison's brows knit together. "An appointment? Why?"

Olivia sucked in a deep breath. This was it. She had to fess up. Level with him. "After Christmas with your mom and seeing Payton the baby-making machine, I just…I *needed* to try and have a baby, Jamison. For *both* of us. I decided to go ahead with another in vitro procedure on my own."

Jamison's confused expression deepened. "Exactly what are you saying?"

"It's pretty simple. Except, actually, it's not. When I went in for the appointment—on that day right there—" she pointed to the photos and grimaced at him, making it clear that they'd revisit the issue of the P.I. photos "—Dr. Demetrios delivered news I didn't want to hear. He told me that tests proved that my body is going through early menopause, and most likely, that's why we're having trouble conceiving. He said that there was a very limited opportunity left for me to get pregnant. So, as you can imagine, I was quite upset. When I ran out of his office, he came after me in the parking lot because he didn't want me to drive. Sure, he hugged me— that's what you're seeing there. He was comforting me—as my brothers might have comforted me. There certainly wasn't anything illicit going on. Believe me."

Jamison stared at the photo for a moment.

"Why didn't you tell me, Liv?" His voice was so soft it was almost a whisper.

"I tried, but you didn't return my calls."

"Oh, my God." He raked a hand over his anguished face and sighed a miserable sigh. "I am so sorry."

"Jamison, look at me."

He did. Square in the eyes. With their gazes locked, she said, "There has never been another man for me. Never has, never will be. I love *you.*"

He got up and went over to her, sat next to her and pulled her close.

As he kissed her tenderly, first her lips, then her neck and her collarbones, she decided that there was no need to rake him over the coals over having her followed. She had nothing to hide. She'd told him everything…and now she wanted to give him everything.

He'd never felt such overwhelming relief in his entire life. Deep inside he'd known Olivia was true to their marriage, to *him,* but he hadn't realized just how afraid he was to lose her.

He felt as if he'd been given a second chance, a new lease on life, on their marriage, and he was so overwhelmingly happy that they'd wiped the slate clean, that they were starting over.

He wanted to show her how much he'd ached for her, how much he'd missed her and longed for this reunion. He wanted to show her with his lips and hands and body why he was the only man for her.

Right there in the living room, on the chintz couch, she responded as he held her and touched her and tasted her. In response his own body swelled and hardened. He loved the feel of her slight body, so fragile to his touch. When he moved his hands to her hips, cupping her body and pulling her closer, she arched against him, firing the hardness of his desire.

"I've missed you so much," she murmured breathlessly.

He raised his hands to her small breasts, cupping them through her thin sweater, savoring their slight curves before teasing her hard nipples. She gasped. Her head fell back and she seemed to lose herself in his touch.

But only for a moment when she slid her hand down the front of his trousers and claimed his erection. Over and over she teased him, rubbing and stroking his desire through the layers of his wool pants and briefs. It had been so long and the sensation was almost too much to bear.

He wanted to savor this moment. So, he took her hands in his and eased her down on the couch, kissing her throat and playfully biting down on her earlobe as he did.

The thought of making love to her sent a hungry shudder racking his whole body. Suddenly he needed her naked so that he could bury himself inside of her. *Now.*

When he pushed up her skirt up around her waist, he saw that she was wearing a garter belt and stockings. The sexy sight of her almost undid him.

She must have sensed as much, because she reached up and unbuttoned his pants. She slid down the zipper and he moved so that she could push his pants down so that he was free.

It felt like the first time again. Wanting to savor the moment, he slowed down and undid each button on his shirt, shrugging it aside so that it dropped to the floor. In one swift, gentle motion, he lifted her so that he could remove her buttery soft sweater.

She lay beneath him in her bra and stockings looking like a slice of heaven. He must have been crazy to have thought they needed time apart.

Slowly, he unhooked the front clasp on her bra. As he freed her breasts, he lowered his head and, in turn, took each one into his mouth, suckling until she cried out in pleasure. As they lay together naked, despite the need driving him to the edge of madness, again, he purposely slowed down, taking a moment to drink in the way her beautiful body looked and to bask in how much he loved her.

And then they were reaching for each other and kissing each other deeply, body to body, skin to skin, tongues thrusting, hands exploring, teeth nipping— hungrily devouring each other. As he buried himself inside her, he knew without a doubt that this was where he wanted to be, where he needed to be. Because their time apart had proved that life was nothing without her.

Chapter Ten

A few hours later, Jamison awoke with Olivia in his arms. It was so good to be lying here next to her, back in his own bed, making love to his wife.

Somehow, they'd found their way up to the bedroom, stopping to make love on the staircase, in the hall and finally on the bed.

Then they did it again.

Olivia shifted, stretched and snuggled closer to him. He buried his nose in her hair, breathing in the floral fragrance of her shampoo and the notes that were uniquely her mingling with the scent of their lovemaking. It was enough to make him crazy. He wanted her so much, he got hard simply thinking about it.

He kissed her neck and, when she stirred and kissed him back, he tried to shift her on top of him, but she resisted.

"What time is it?" Her voice was husky with sleep.

"Ten-fifteen." He breathed the words into her ear and again she moved so that her body spooned perfectly with his, her tight little rump teasing his erection.

"Aren't you hungry?" she asked.

"I'm ravenous." He nudged her, wanting to part her legs and slip inside her warmth, but she turned and faced him, just out of reach.

He moaned and she ran her finger along his jawline.

"I ordered us a feast from Juan Carlo's. Endive salad with blue cheese, walnuts and honey, stuffed dates, salmon with crème fraîche and caviar, beef skewers, and cream of artichoke soup, with chocolate fondue for dessert. Plus, we need to open that bottle of champagne that's been waiting for us since Christmas Eve."

She started to get out of bed, but he pulled her back down on top of him.

"I'm starving, but not for food." He trailed kisses down her neck and chest to her breasts. Then he gently took her nipple between his teeth.

Her soft moan stoked the fire, and he sucked her

breast into his mouth. She felt so small and fragile in his arms, which, in turn spawned a protectiveness that he hadn't felt in a very long time. But when he looked up, the resolve in her eyes reinforced the strength of her determined spirit, which she demonstrated as she smiled, pushed away from him and got out of bed.

"Come help me," she said. "We can put the food in a picnic basket and bring it up here. We can have a feast in bed. Who knows what we might do with that chocolate fondue…for dessert."

She crooked her finger and beckoned him to follow. He was trailing after her in a flash.

Before too long, they were back upstairs, with their gourmet picnic spread out around them on the bed.

Jamison popped the cork on the champagne, and Olivia held out two flutes.

"Are you drinking?" he asked.

"Well, yes. Why?"

"You were always so adamant about staying away from alcohol in the weeks before you had the in vitro procedure. We are going to try again, aren't we? Because since you went to see the doctor, I'm guessing you've already started the hormones, right? If I learned one thing—no, two things—while we were apart it's that I love you very much and that I'm ready to start our family. Olivia, I think we need this to complete us. And with your condition, it sounds like we don't have any time to waste. I love you, and I want you to have my baby."

Olivia's gaze searched her husband's face as the implication of his words sank in.

I love you, and I want you to have my baby.

Finally, he was ready.

But this was just as she'd learned that her only option for getting pregnant was the donor eggs. And she hadn't told him that part. Mainly because she didn't know how to.

It was never so apparent that they needed a child to keep them together. If she couldn't give him that, it might spell the end of their marriage.

She would do anything to keep them together.

Technically, even with a donor egg, she would be having *his* baby. His sperm would fertilize the donor egg. And as Derek said, no one need be the wiser.

Even so, her conscience niggled at her. She tried to stave off black clouds of doubt by reminding herself that in a roundabout way, their situation was similar to Paul and Ramona's ordeal. Not literally, of course, but loosely, in the same way that Ramona had deceived Paul, but he'd forgiven her.

Ramona's mother had needed a bone marrow transplant, and Ramona had been desperate to find someone who was a match. She'd learned that years ago, her mom had donated eggs to the Armstrong Institute. Going on a hunch, Ramona had taken a job as a PR specialist at the institute to gain access to the files to see if she could find out if anyone had delivered a baby using her mother's eggs. A child with her mother's own DNA, who might be the answer to her prayers.

Unbeknownst to anyone, she was also on assignment for *Keeping Up With Medicine.* The journal had hired her to write an exposé on the institute as she searched the files for the identity of the recipient of her mother's eggs. Sure she'd written the damning story, but she'd tried to pull it before it went to press. Her editor had acted against Ramona's wishes, publishing the story anyway.

Ramona had initially deceived Paul for the greater good of her family, and once the truth—and why she'd done it—was out in the open, their relationship had not only survived, it thrived. Not immediately, of course. They'd had to mend and heal their trust. But love had triumphed.

If there was one thing Olivia still believed in, it was the power of her and Jamison's love.

As he toasted her and their family-to-be, she resolved to do whatever it took to give her husband the family they both so desperately wanted. She'd come this far, she couldn't give up now. Because what else would she have left if she lost him? She'd given up ballet and a career of her own to foster *his* career and nurture their family. If she didn't deliver her end of the bargain and give Jamison that family, she'd lose him. She couldn't afford to let any options slip by untried.

Three weeks later Jamison held her hand at the institute as Dr. Chance Demetrios implanted three fertilized embryos into Olivia's body.

Now, they simply had to sit back and wait to see if the procedure took.

After the procedure, she encouraged him to go back to D.C. He couldn't spend the entire nine months holding her hand—or even the agonizing two weeks she had to wait before she could get the pregnancy blood tests. Olivia might have felt desperate, but she never, ever wanted to be perceived that way.

So she insisted that he go back to work while she busied herself at the Children's Home. Staying busy would keep both their minds off whether the procedure had taken hold.

Dr. Demetrios had told her not to even bother with over-the-counter home pregnancy tests because, this early in the game, more often than not, they gave false negative results. So, her only recourse was to get lost in her work at the home.

Pam needed plenty of help with the Kelso boys. Not that they were difficult, although the little one, because of his autism, did need extra help—which he didn't always want. Danny often insisted that only his brother could help him, which posed a problem now that the holidays were over and Kevin had returned to school.

Pam and Olivia had established with Kevin's school that he could finish out the year even though the Children's Home was out of the district. The routine and familiarity would be good for him, considering all the drastic changes in his life. The only drawback was that the county could not provide school bus transportation for him. Someone had to drive him, and Olivia had decided that someone would be her.

This morning when she walked into the Children's Home, the mansion's spacious living room had been restored to rights, the Christmas decorations put back in storage. The first thing she saw was Danny sitting in a corner alone, rolling something between his thumb and his first two fingers.

When Olivia went over to see what he had, she realized that the small, white object was one of the pearls that had fallen to the ground the day the necklace broke.

NANCY ROBARDS THOMPSON   141

When she'd picked up the repaired necklace from the jewelers, it had felt a bit snug. Olivia had had no idea how many pearls were on the strand, so maybe the necklace felt shorter because there was a pearl missing?

She knelt down in front of the small boy. "Hi, Danny. What do you have there? May I see it?"

"Duck," he quacked. "Duck. Duck. Duck!"

Olivia had done some research on autism and discovered that often a child afflicted with the condition would fixate on a certain object and assign it a name that had nothing to do with it. Just as Danny called her pearl a duck.

It was unfortunate that Danny had fixated on her pearl. He was only three years old and if he put it in his mouth, he might choke on it.

"Sweetie, could I please have that?" Olivia tried to take it from his little hand. Not only did he refuse to let go, but he started screaming at the top of his lungs.

Kevin was at his side in a flash.

"What are you doing to him?" Kevin demanded.

"I'm trying to take that bead away from him," she said over the screams. "I'm afraid he might swallow it."

Olivia noticed that Kevin didn't touch Danny or even try to comfort him. Instead, he'd assumed a protective stance between Danny and Olivia, and verbally took up his younger brother's battle.

"He won't put it in his mouth," Kevin said. "He

never does that, but he won't stop screaming if you keep trying to take it from him."

Kevin seemed totally unfazed by his little brother's ruckus, but it was all Olivia could do to keep from covering her ears with her hands.

Pam rushed into the room, her eyes bright with alarm. "What's wrong?"

"Danny has a bead and I tried to take from him because I don't want him to put it in his mouth. He didn't like it."

"Yeah," Kevin chimed in. "I told you he'll pretty much scream until he thinks he's safe and that you're not going to take it away from him."

Pam shot Olivia a frazzled, worried, what-are-we-going-to-do look as the other Children's Home residents started to gather around to see what all the fuss was about.

"Well, he has to learn that he won't get his way just because he screams. Everyone has to abide by certain rules."

Kevin shrugged, as if he couldn't understand what all the fuss was about.

"It's not like he's going to try and eat it or anything. He just likes it because it makes him feel safe."

Kevin's sage insight made Olivia catch her breath. The little guy was wise beyond his years.

Pam took a step forward and frowned. "Is that one of your pearls?"

Olivia shrugged. "All I'm concerned about is his safety. I don't want him to put it in his mouth and swallow it."

Pam frowned. "Danny, give me the bead, please. It doesn't belong to you."

The boy screamed louder. Pam and Olivia offered him a succession of toys, to no avail. Danny held tight to the pearl, continuing to scream when they tried unsuccessfully to pry it from his grip.

Pam turned to Olivia. "What in the world am I going to do?"

Olivia understood Pam's dilemma, but at the same time, her heart was breaking for this poor little guy who was barely out of the toddler phase of his life and for his brave, older brother, who was also much too young to be all alone in the world at the tender age of seven.

All Danny wanted was to feel safe. Olivia wished there was some way she could comfort him. But she knew that sometimes all the pearls in the world—all the things that money could buy—could never take the place of a family.

Something Kevin said kept going through her head. *"He just likes it because it makes him feel safe."*

As she racked her brain for a solution and came

up short, suddenly she saw Kevin standing next to Pam holding a large toy dump truck. He started spinning the shiny wheels around and around.

"Look, Danny," he said. "Truck! *Vroom! Vroom vroom! Vroom vroom vroom! Truck!*"

The little boy stopped screaming. His gaze fixed on the spinning wheels. He didn't say anything, but he stared at the truck for a long moment before reaching for it. When Kevin handed it to him, the single pearl Danny had been holding fell to the floor, bouncing as it did.

Pam caught it on the up-bounce, closing her hand around it before stashing it out of sight in her pocket.

"I'll give it back to you later," she whispered to Olivia.

Olivia smiled. "No worries. I know where you live." Danny plopped down in the center of the living room and spun the truck wheels. The only evidence of his earlier outburst was his tearstained face. Satisfied that the boy the was fine, Olivia said, "Come on, Kevin. Let's get you to school."

When they were in the car, they rode in silence for a few moments. When they reached a stoplight, Olivia said, "Kevin, that was a wonderful thing you did, figuring out how to help your little brother."

The boy stared straight ahead and shrugged, a quick, it-was-nothing hitch of the shoulders.

"I mean it," Olivia said. "Pam and I didn't know what to do. We didn't know how to help him, but you did."

The boy looked up at her, his expression very matter of fact. "He likes shiny things. Not all shiny things, but I thought he'd like the truck because he likes shiny things that spin around."

Olivia nodded. "He's so lucky to have a big brother like you."

Kevin's face clouded and he turned away and looked out the window. "Are you really going to make me and Danny go live in separate houses with different families?"

The question knocked the air out of Olivia. "What makes you ask that, Kevin?"

Another quick rise and fall of the shoulders.

The light turned green and Olivia drove through the intersection with a death grip on the steering wheel.

"The kids said you're gonna send me and Danny far away from each other and we wouldn't be brothers anymore."

This time, his sad words forced a gasp from Olivia.

"Oh, sweetie, have they really been saying that?"

She slanted a glance at him in time to catch his quick nod. In turn, she steered the car into the first parking lot she came to—a doughnut shop. As she put the car in park, she weighed her words. The sad truth of the matter was that she couldn't guarantee that the boys wouldn't be adopted out to different families. She didn't want to lie to him, but when she looked into his haunted brown eyes, she knew she couldn't tell him that the chances of them going to the same family were very slim.

"Kevin, you and Danny will always be brothers. And I want you to know that Pam will do everything in her power to keep the two of you together. Okay?"

He didn't say a word. He simply sat stock still, staring out the side window. The sight of him broke her heart.

Say something to make him feel better, she chided herself. She glared at the neon sign of the doughnut shop. She couldn't just blow sunshine at him, because if her thin promises ended up falling through, they would do more damage to him than the moment of temporary happiness she'd manufacture right now was worth.

"I'm really hungry," she finally said. "Will you go into the doughnut shop with me so that I can get a snack?"

Kevin nodded solemnly.

"Okay then," Olivia said. "Let's go."

* * *

On the way back to the house, Olivia called Jamison.

"Good morning," he said.

"Good morning," she returned. "Do you have a moment?"

"For you, I have all the time in the world."

His voice made Olivia smile as she turned the car onto Berkeley Street.

"I have a nearly impossible task that I need your help with," she said. "In fact, it's a cause so important to me that I'm going to be rallying everyone I know. Jamison, we have to find a good family that would be willing to adopt the Kelso boys. Both of them. How do we do that?"

Chapter Eleven

Later that month, Jamison and Olivia attended a reception following the President's State of the Union address in Washington, D.C. It was their first official public appearance as a couple since the trial separation, and at functions like this, it was so clear why they were good together.

Olivia knew how to charm the crowd. Seeing her in action, he knew that someday, she'd make a perfect first lady—that the country would fall in love with her as deeply as he had.

As he stood listening to a junior congressman who was concerned about the direction of one of the committees Jamison chaired, he watched his wife across the room.

She wore her brunette hair twisted up off her neck, adding to the elegance of her black dress and pearls.

She'd been working tirelessly trying to find the Kelso boys a home together. In turn, she'd been spending every spare minute that she was at home in Boston with them. If it wasn't that she seemed so happy lately, he might worry that she was getting too attached to them herself.

But then again, that was his wife. Always putting her heart and soul into everything she took on, always looking for the win-win solution. Another case in point of why she'd be a good first lady—she was the ultimate humanitarian.

Tonight, she seemed to glow from within as never before. Their gazes snagged and held for a moment. He could read the "I'm ready to leave whenever you are" look in her dark eyes, even though the message would've been missed by anyone else. Even in a crowd they'd always been able to communicate wordlessly across the room.

Jamison smiled at her and the congressman stopped mid-sentence and turned to see who he was looking at.

"Gorgeous, isn't she?" the congressman said. "I noticed her earlier tonight during the President's address."

Jamison snickered. "Did you?"

The other man nodded.

"That's my wife," Jamison said. "I'm glad you approve."

The young man's eyes widened. "I hope I didn't offend you. It's just that she's stunning. I couldn't help but notice her because she's the spitting image of Audrey Hepburn. You're one lucky man."

"Indeed, I am," Jamison said. He excused himself and made his way over to Olivia, who was just finishing a conversation with a former first lady.

When there was a break in the conversation, Jamison whispered to his wife, "Come on, let's get out of here." He whisked Olivia away, helped her into her coat, and hand in hand they walked outside to the waiting limousine. After they were settled in the car, he said, "Was she giving you pointers for 2016?"

Jamison put his arm around her and pulled her in close.

Olivia smiled up at him and his heart turned over in response. How did he get so lucky to be blessed with her? They may have had their ups and downs, but they always rebounded, stronger every time.

"She was lovely," Olivia said. "Very warm. And so interesting."

He rested his chin on top of her fragrant hair,

loving the feel of her tucked in so close to him. "Of course, you could probably teach her a thing or two."

She laughed, tilting her face up so that he was able to capture her lips with his. She tasted faintly of mint, and a lingering honeyed sweetness that made him thirst for more.

"I don't think there was a head in that room that didn't turn when you walked by." His voice was a hoarse whisper. "I had to get you out of there before someone decided to steal you away."

She shook her head, a seductive smile coaxing up the corners of her mouth.

"Really?" she said. "What on earth would anyone else want with a powerful political gentleman's pregnant wife?"

Jamison blinked, unsure that he'd heard her correctly, but cautiously optimistic. "Are you saying what I think you're saying?"

"I'm pregnant, Jamison. Dr. Demetrios confirmed it this morning. I wasn't going to tell you until we were back at the apartment, but I couldn't wait another minute."

His mouth fell open, but too many emotions were converging for him to say anything.

"Can you believe it?" she said, smiling. "This time, I really believe everything is going to be okay."

He hugged her and kissed her tenderly on the lips.

Feeling like a protective papa bear, he said, "But should you have flown today? Will the air pressure hurt the baby?"

She shook her head. "That's one of the first things I asked the doctor. He said I'd be fine. He said it was important for me to keep doing all the things I normally do. To be careful of adding too many new things, but that I should live life as normally as possible."

He gazed down at her, thinking that in the amber glow of the street she was the most beautiful woman in the world. Not only was she beautiful, but she was giving him the best gift a wife could ever give her husband. She was having his baby. How could he have doubted that he wanted this? It was simply fear of the unknown. Fear that a baby would change them, when in reality Olivia had been right, a baby seemed to be exactly what they needed.

"Liv, I want you to stay with me here in D.C. I don't want us to be apart. I want to take care of you. I want to experience every stage of our baby growing inside of you."

"But, Jamison, my doctor is in Boston. I just don't think it would work."

Of course he wanted what was best for the baby, but he also wanted his wife.

"I need you by my side," he said. "When is your next doctor's appointment?"

"Two weeks."

"How about this? Why don't you stay in D.C. with me until your next appointment and then let's see what Dr. Demetrios says. If he thinks it's safe for you to move down here with me, then maybe he could refer you to a specialist."

The look on her face hinted that she wanted to say yes, but something was troubling her.

"What is it, Liv?"

She sighed. "It's the boys—Danny and Kevin. I can't just abandon them, Jamison."

It was getting easier to forget that the child growing inside her wasn't really hers. Part of it was because she already felt attached to the baby. Another reason was her rationalization that what she'd done couldn't be too terribly wrong since the pregnancy had taken and seemed to be thriving. Even she had to admit that she had a glow about her. She looked and felt good. Better, in fact, than she had in years. Not even a hint of morning sickness.

Curious as to why this pregnancy seemed to be working while the others with her own eggs hadn't, she'd done some research. Apparently, in early onset menopause sometimes the eggs could be damaged or not as high quality as those from a woman whose body was more typically in tune with her chronological age. There was no way she could confirm this with her doctor since he had no idea that the eggs he'd implanted weren't really hers, but it made sense.

And if this pregnancy gave them their child, well, then this was the child—the gift from God—that they were meant to receive.

Jamison seemed so earnest when he asked her to move to D.C. with him. After she thought about it— and received the all clear from her doctor, who had no objections as long as she was able to make it back for her checkups—she couldn't deny her husband. Things were going so well with them, and she wanted that time with him. Though the time apart had made them realize how much they loved each other, it was the time together that was helping to heal and nurture them as a couple and move them forward into this next exciting chapter of their life.

There would've been no question about what she should do, if not for Danny and Kevin. But Jamison had been right when he reminded her that the boys were in good hands with Pam. Still, Olivia felt an overwhelming need to see them and explain to Kevin that even though she'd be away and visiting less frequently, she'd still be there for them.

It was an eight-hour train ride—and even faster by plane, she told herself as she arranged the football and new toy truck she'd gotten them on the backseat of the car. She'd grown so close to the boys since they'd arrived at the Children's Home, and she couldn't help this urge she felt to shower them with love—and gifts—so that they knew that they weren't alone in the world.

Kevin greeted her enthusiastically and helped her buckle Danny, who was clutching his dump truck, into the car seat that had become a permanent fixture in the back of her Jaguar.

"Who does *that* belong to?" he asked, eyeing the football.

Olivia smiled at him. "Oh, goodness, how did that get in my car?" She winked at him. "I don't suppose you know anyone who'd like to have that, would you?"

The boy beamed and hugged the ball to his chest. Danny was less excited about the new truck, clinging to the tried and true dump truck for which he'd traded in his pearl. But that was okay. Kevin's gusto was enough.

Today, she was taking them to Public Gardens. It had become one of their favorite spots—even in the cold of winter. Today she'd packed a thermos of homemade hot chocolate and a batch of freshly baked cookies. Sometimes on weekends, when it wasn't too cold, they'd bring a picnic and find a patch of sunshine where they could spread their blanket and eat their lunch. Other times, they'd seat

Danny in an umbrella stroller and she and Kevin would walk the grounds. This, she'd discovered, was the best way to get the older boy to open up. And he would, sometimes going on for a solid hour about his friends at school, his teacher and the classes he loved most. But never a word about his parents or his feelings about the tragic loss he'd suffered.

Olivia didn't push him. She figured he'd open up in good time—if he wanted to. All that was important now was that he always seemed glad to see her.

When they got to the park, Kevin asked, "Do you know how to throw a football, Olivia?"

"No, I don't. Will you teach me?"

He tried his best. While Danny sat on the blanket bundled up in his winter coat spinning the wheels of his truck, Kevin and Olivia tossed the football. She dropped it more than she caught it, she wasn't able to throw the ball into the distance when he ran long, and she broke two fingernails, but she tried her hardest. Even so, Kevin seemed to tire of her efforts quickly and decided he needed to check on Danny.

They sat down on the blanket and she poured him a cup of hot chocolate.

"Why don't you offer Danny a cookie?" Olivia suggested. "He can eat that while his cocoa cools."

Olivia's heart swelled as she watched the younger boy respond to his older brother and take the cookie.

It was such a beautiful moment. What a shame that she'd have to spoil it with the news that she was leaving, but she needed to tell him while they were sitting here. She dreaded it, but the longer she put it off the harder it would be.

"Sorry I'm not very good at football," Olivia said, buying a little more time.

The boy lifted one shoulder to his ear and let it fall, then stared down at the football in his lap. "It's okay. My mom wasn't very good at it, either. It was something my dad and me used to do together."

Olivia's skin prickled. It was the first time he'd ever mentioned his parents. She wondered whether her telling him that she was leaving would affect his progress. On one hand, his opening up could mean that he was starting to adjust to his new environment. On the other, her leaving might cause him to retreat back into his shell.

I can't leave him now.

The possibility danced through her mind, but she shoved it out as quickly as it appeared. Jamison and the baby were her family. As much as she loved the Kelso boys, her family had to be her first priority.

Still, it didn't erase the sick feeling of dread that washed over her.

She reached out and smoothed his bangs off his forehead, relishing the silky softness of them.

"You miss your parents, don't you?"

He nodded, still not looking at her.

"It's okay, Kevin. You know that Mr. Mallory and I are here for you, don't you?"

He bobbed his head again, just barely this time.

"I wanted to let you know that I'm going away for a couple of weeks, but I'll be back."

Kevin looked up at her, alarm widening his chocolate brown eyes. "That's what my mommy told me and she never came back."

"Oohh…" Olivia choked back a sob. "Come here, sweetheart."

She pulled the boy onto her lap and held him tight for a long moment. He didn't cry, but he held on to her as if she were his lifeline.

"I'll see you again in two weeks. And when we get home, I'll mark the days on a calendar for you so that you can see exactly how quickly I'll be back. Would that make you feel better?"

The boy didn't answer her. He simply tightened his hold on her. Olivia sat there, hugging him back.

"If it would make you feel better, I'll call you every day after school so that you can tell me about your day. Would you like that?"

Still no answer.

"I'll even give you my cell phone number so that you can call me whenever you'd like to talk. Because

I want you to know that Mr. Mallory and I will do anything in the world for you and Danny."

The boy released his grip and looked up at her.

"Anything?" he asked.

Olivia nodded. "Anything. You can call me anytime of the day or night."

"Will you take Danny and me with you? Will you be our new mommy?"

Jamison went with Olivia to her next prenatal appointment, which happened to be on Valentine's Day. The best Valentine she could've ever asked for was to get the news that she'd checked out fine, that the baby was growing and that everything seemed to be textbook perfect. They celebrated with lunch at Salvatore's down on Boston's South Port waterfront.

After ordering lunch—Jamison chose the lobster ravioli and her mouth watered in anticipation of their famous salad with gorgonzola, walnuts and green apples—he presented her with a pearl bracelet from Tiffany's. It had a heart-shaped diamond dangling from the clasp.

"Oh, Jamison, it's gorgeous. Thank you."

He smiled. "I thought it was significant. The diamond represents our baby. Just don't wear it around your little friend with the pearl obsession."

The thought made Olivia smile, too, as she slipped the bracelet on her arm. She missed her little guys. She hadn't seen them in two weeks. Two weeks during which Kevin's question had haunted her—"Will you be our new mommy?"

She'd managed to sidestep the little boy's question by using the excuse that he and Danny couldn't come with her to D.C. because Kevin had to go to school. She told him that she wished it were as easy as agreeing to be his new mommy, but that the situation was...complicated.

He had no idea exactly how complicated it really was.

The excuses hadn't meant anything to him, and Olivia saw him cry for the first time when she marked off the days she'd be gone on his calendar and said goodbye to him and promised him she'd come see him her first day back.

Actually, she didn't know who the farewell was harder on—Kevin...or her.

"How do you tell a little boy like Kevin Kelso that you can't be his mother?" she asked Jamison. "He's only seven years old. He's smart as can be, but it won't make it any easier on him to tell him I would if I could, but I can't. All he'll hear is, 'No' and he'll feel like he's lost someone he cares about all over again."

"Are you going to regret getting involved with the boys?" Jamison asked.

Olivia paused, fork midair and gaped at her husband. "Of course not."

Jamison cut another bite of ravioli. "I didn't think so. So don't be so hard on yourself, Liv. You're giving them a lot right now, when he and Danny need you the most."

He popped the bite into his mouth. Olivia sighed and set down her fork. "What I'm saying is that I don't want to cause him further pain. He doesn't know that we're going to have a baby of our own. He won't give a flip that we need this time for our own family. He'll feel as if we rejected him."

Jamison sipped his iced tea. "I don't know, Liv. He sounds like a pretty resilient little guy to me. I'm sure he'll be okay. Just because we can't adopt him and Danny doesn't mean that you can't continue to see them. Probably even after they're adopted by another family."

"Why can't we adopt them, Jamison?" She startled herself with the question. Where had it come from?

She was just opening her mouth to retract the question, when Jamison said, "One reason I can think of is because I've never even met them. I mean, I feel as if I know them since you talk about them so much, but you know, hey, we've never actually met."

The realization hit Olivia like a bolt. It had been nearly two months that she'd been talking about them, but, no, he *hadn't* met them.

"How about if I come by the Children's Home with you?"

It was a great idea. They had just enough time to do that and then get back to the house so that they could get ready for dinner with their families. Even though she was only about six weeks along, they couldn't wait to share their news—especially after the good checkup earlier that day.

Jamison had left the decision of when to share the good news up to her and she'd felt confident about making the announcement tonight. This time, it just felt different. But first, she had an introduction to make. The three most important men in her life had to meet each other.

Jamison steered Olivia's Jaguar into the parking lot of the Children's Home. She held his hand and led him up the steps.

After they were buzzed in, Olivia immediately set out to look for Pam and the little boys who had so captured her heart.

Jamison stepped into the living room and knew from the description that Olivia had given him that he'd stumbled upon one of them. He'd heard so much about these boys he felt as if he already knew them. He'd bet money that this was Danny, who sat quietly in the corner, spinning the wheel of a toy truck.

Jamison walked over and knelt in front of him.

"Hi there, little guy. What do you have there?"

The boy didn't say anything, and for a long while, Jamison would've sworn that the kid didn't even know he was there. That's why he was surprised when, as he started to get up, the boy held out the truck and let Jamison take it.

The moment after Jamison accepted it he didn't quite know what to do with it. Should he roll it on the ground? Should he make truck noises? He didn't want the boy to start screaming again the way Olivia had said he did when someone tried to take his favorite toy. For lack of a better idea of what to do, Jamison gave the wheels a spin, the same way Danny had been doing when Jamison entered the room.

The boy stared transfixed. Once Jamison saw the boy was okay with sharing his truck, he relaxed and both of them fell into a contented companionship with each other. Though he knew feeling sorry for him was probably the worst thing he could do for the boy, he couldn't help but be moved by the fact that the kid was so young to be without his family.

Despite how Jamison had all the material advantages money could buy, thanks to an absent father and a mother who was an emotional wreck, his child-hood had been less than ideal. Even so, he had his *people*. He'd always had his brothers around him.

Sitting here with Danny, recalling everything Olivia had said, he fully understood why it was so important to keep these boys together.

When Olivia, Pam and another boy, who had to be Kevin because he looked like a slightly larger version of Danny, walked in, they stopped in their tracks and gaped at them as if they were afraid that they might startle a wild deer.

"He shared his truck with you?" asked Kevin.

"He shared his truck with you," Olivia said.

"He shared his truck with me." Jamison beamed.

He'd been with the little guy for less than fifteen minutes and he could already see why Olivia was so smitten. If it wasn't that he and his wife already had a baby on the way, he'd definitely entertain the pos-sibility that the boys come live with Olivia and him.

But that was impulse talking. Jamison had just met the boys. He hadn't even spent time with them. Even if did and fell in love with them the same way Olivia had, it wouldn't work. It would simply be too much for Olivia to care for a newborn and two emotionally fragile older boys—especially one with special needs.

Particularly since Jamison would be so busy with work.

His own childhood flashed back at him in one, larger than life mental collage of lies and deception. Six little boys who desperately needed a father. A father who was never there for them. A mother who was so overwhelmed by the fact that her marriage was unraveling that she drank herself into a stupor on a regular basis.

There were so many unanswered questions and the memory sent a steel door slamming down on Jamison's overloaded emotions.

As much as he was sure the boys were wonderful and worthy of love and a good home, he and Olivia simply weren't their new family. It would be too much. Overload. Somehow, he had to make Olivia see that.

Chapter Twelve

"It was a sign that he is going to be a great father," Olivia said to the group of family gathered around the dining room table at their house. "Danny was drawn to Jamison. And in the time I've known him, I've never seen him share with anyone that way."

"Who, Danny or Jamison?" Paul asked, and everyone at the table doubled over in a fit of laughter.

"Danny, of course." Olivia reached for her husband's hand.

"Right, because Jamison hasn't learned to share yet. I think the three-year-old is setting a good example,"

Paul continued, and drew more laughter. Jamison was a good sport and chuckled along with them.

"This evening was not intended to be a roast honoring my husband," Olivia said. "But we do have some very exciting news to share. In fact, if not for this news, we might even consider adopting the Kelso boys, we've come to care for them that much. But one thing at a time."

As the server they'd hired for the evening distributed flutes of champagne—and a glass of sparkling cider for Olivia—she beamed at her husband, who seemed to be in a daze and frowning slightly. When she raised her glass to him he seemed to snap out of his fog. Because he smiled, she decided not to read anything into it.

This is a happy night. Don't borrow trouble.

"Jamison, would you please do the honor and share our good news with our family?"

Olivia's mother, Emily Stanton Armstrong, seemed to anticipate the announcement and gasped. Her hand flew to her mouth as if she were holding in the happy, hopeful question that wanted to pop out.

In turn, Emily's reaction elicited a muffled squeal from Olivia's sister, Lisa. "Oh, I hope you're going to say what I think you're going to say."

Jamison's mother, Helen, sat poker-faced in her seat to the right of her son, who was at the head of the table.

"Oh, for God's sake," she hissed. "Would everyone be quiet so he can talk?"

Jamison cleared his throat, a sign that his mother's brusque manners had embarrassed him.

"Relax, Mother. I'm waiting until everyone has been served champagne."

Helen gave an aloof half-eye roll that might have been a smirk, but it was hard to tell.

"Oh, smile," cajoled Olivia's father, Gerald. "You're actually quite attractive when you do."

Emily and Helen glared at Gerald, who, in his day had quite a reputation for being a womanizer. But Olivia knew he'd changed his ways and truly loved her mother. She knew her father was a good man, even if she'd never been as close to him as to her mother.

Every single member of Olivia's family was present tonight. Derek was a bit subdued, but he'd come. Paul had even brought his fiancée, Ramona.

Olivia was overjoyed they were all there, because nothing made her quite as happy as being surrounded by her family.

Helen, however, was the only member of Jamison's family who could make it tonight. Four of his brothers lived out of town; Payton and Grant had their own Valentine's Day plans, which was understandable, and actually preferable to Olivia. Because invariably, Payton would've found some way to upstage their announcement.

Olivia shook away the ugly thought. She wasn't going to let anything spoil the night. Especially not ugly thoughts aimed at a sister-in-law, whose only faults, really, were being impossibly fertile and well liked by their mother-in-law.

Olivia was neither of those things.

Still, this was her and Jamison's night. A time to enjoy their family and bask in the glow of the happy news they were about to share.

When everybody had flutes of champagne, Jamison sat up straight and said, "Olivia and I are very happy to announce that we are expecting a baby, which will arrive in October."

Shouts and squeals erupted. The family toasted and hugged one another as they congratulated Olivia and Jamison. Olivia even thought she saw evidence of a smile on Helen's face—but it was gone before she could be sure.

When everyone settled down, Helen said, "October? That means you aren't even two months' pregnant, Olivia. Don't you think it's a bit risky to start making announcements this early?"

A hush fell over the dining room and everyone

gaped as Helen's thoughtless remark loomed, almost palpable, in the air.

"The doctor said that everything looks good, Mother." There was a sharp edge to Jamison's voice. "Besides, we're going to be spending a lot of time in D.C. over the coming months. Tonight was the most convenient night to get the family together, seeing that you happened to be in town tonight, too. Perhaps you could think positively and wish us well?"

"Of course," Helen said, then downed the rest of her champagne.

In an awkward moment, all gazes seemed to turn to Olivia. She wasn't sure if the crushing weight she felt was due to the hormones or simply disappointment that even on the night she announced she was finally pregnant, she couldn't seem to please her mother-in-law, who had to spoil the moment by shining the spotlight on Olivia's worst nightmare—that they might possibly lose the baby. Again.

She hated it, but she felt tears burning her eyes. There was no way she was going to let Helen know she'd gotten to her. No way she was going to sit her and cry and validate her mother-in-law's morbid suggestion.

Olivia summoned her most cheerful voice.

"If you'll excuse me, I'll just go into the kitchen and let the staff know that we're ready for dessert."

As the servers bustled around her, Olivia stood in her kitchen struggling to regain her composure. She did it by focusing on the good, replaying the wonderful day she'd had in her head—the good news that they'd received at the doctor's appointment; the wonderful lunch with Jamison and the sentimental bracelet he'd given her; the way Danny and Jamison had taken to each other; and now being able to share the good news with the family.

Despite Helen's sourpuss attitude, for once the world really did seem nearly perfect. Olivia put her hand over her stomach, which was still perfectly flat. She couldn't change her mother-in-law's outlook, but she could refuse to let it bring her down. Because, really, the only way life could be better would be if she were holding her baby in her arms right now.

She turned at the sound of someone behind her. It was Derek.

"Is everything okay?" she asked.

"Everything seems fine, my dear sister. Well, except for Helen. She's quite a piece of work, isn't she? But really, you should be quite pleased with yourself for pulling this off."

He patted his stomach. Something in the tone of his voice sent a chill skittering down Olivia's spine.

"Derek, don't start with me. I've had enough drama tonight. Did you need something? Otherwise,

I was just getting ready to go back out and join the family in the dining room. We don't want the ice cream to melt."

He started to say something but stopped. His expression was making her uncomfortable.

"I just felt compelled to ask—aren't you glad you listened to me? Because I'm quite enjoying this little secret we're sharing."

Racking her brain because she didn't quite know what to say to him, she glanced around to make sure nobody had slipped into the kitchen and heard his remark. When she was sure the coast was clear, she lowered her voice to just above a whisper.

"Please don't ever bring that up again. Not even when we're alone, okay?"

He laughed a dry laugh that seemed almost evil.

"No, Olivia, I think we're going to have to talk about it at least one more time."

His comment made her blood run cold.

"What are you getting at, Derek?" she muttered the words through gritted teeth.

"Now is not the appropriate time or place. But we'll talk soon, little sister. We'll talk."

As the celebration wound down, Jamison asked his mother to step into the office for a private word before she left for her hotel. Despite their large home and numerous offers, she never stayed with Jamison and Olivia when she visited.

"What's the matter, son?" she asked.

He knew her too well to believe she was really oblivious to what he wanted to talk about.

"Why did you act that way tonight?"

She blinked. "What on earth do you mean, dear?" She was acting a little too wide-eyed and innocent to be believable.

"You know exactly what I'm saying. At every turn of good news you had something snide to say. With all that Olivia and I have been through, it was pretty awful of you to suggest that it's too early to share the pregnancy with our family. For God's sake, we're not sending out a press release to the general public. This night was to celebrate. Family is supposed to rally around you and build you up. Not tear you down."

Helen's mouth pursed into a thin, flat line and pure venom seemed to pool in her eyes. In the split second before she could blast him with her poison tongue, Jamison held up his hand.

"Don't say a word. You're going to hear me and you'd better take to heart what I have to say. I am sick and tired of you being disrespectful to my wife. You will treat her with respect or you will not be welcome in our home. Do I need to make my point any clearer?"

She glared at him. A slight coloring bloomed on her face, hard and cold as a stone.

Over the years, Jamison had tried to convince Olivia that she shouldn't take his mother's chilly demeanor personally. Helen had never like *any* of the women he or his brother, Grant, had brought home (girlfriends of their four, unmarried younger brothers weren't even on Helen's radar). In fact, it was only after Payton had given her a grandchild that Helen had softened toward her. That gave Jamison hope that one day his mother would open her arms and invite Olivia in, but tonight, he'd officially quit hoping. He was demanding it.

He'd accepted the fact that even if his mother was revered in her social circles—the kind of reverence only afforded those with power and old money—she wasn't nice.

"Mother, I love you. I know that you're fighting your own demons. But you have to understand, the past is gone. Nothing can change it. I'm sorry that Dad hurt you. I'm sorry that he was a rotten father to me and my brothers, but I will no longer let the past rob me of the happiness I deserve. For a while now, I've been questioning whether I even wanted children because I was so afraid I'd end up being like my father—being a horrible, horrible husband. But just today, it dawned on me that I am nothing like him—"

"You are *a lot* like him," Helen spat. He wasn't sure if that was a compliment. "That's why people love you. They see in you everything they wanted to believe about him."

Their gazes locked and at that moment, Jamison saw the tears in his mother's eyes, glimpsed all the hurt and anguish that was bottled under the surface.

"Mom, we cannot let the past keep tearing us apart. Olivia is my wife. She is your daughter-in-law, not your competition. So please show her the respect she deserves."

Later that night, Olivia lay awake next to her husband long after he'd fallen asleep. Derek's words rang in her ears. No matter how she tossed and turned, she couldn't quiet her restless, worried mind.

If she didn't know better, she might think Derek was intending to blackmail her.

Surely not, she told herself as she flipped over onto her back and stared at the ceiling. Her brother was capable of a lot of diabolical things, but extorting a family member?

Surely not.

Even so, his careless remark had uncorked the guilt she'd managed to suppress during this time of happiness and celebration.

She turned back onto her side, facing her husband.

His handsome face looked so peaceful and relaxed in the sliver of moonlight that shone through the space in the curtain.

Maybe she should tell him the complete truth.

A wave of panic threatened to drown her.

How could she? He was so happy. They were doing so well.

Again, she flopped onto her back, lacing her hands over her stomach.

How could she possibly keep the secret of using donor eggs from Jamison? Especially if there was a chance Derek was going to spill the beans.

But Derek would have to come up to D.C. if he wanted to have the discussion he seemed so dead set on having. Because she'd decided that's where she was going to be spending most of her time until the baby was born. It wasn't what she wanted—especially because it meant leaving Danny and Kevin again—but putting a safe buffer of four hundred and fifty miles between her and her brother seemed like the best survival tactic right now.

If nothing else, it would force Derek to really think about his actions.

Wouldn't it?

Even though Jamison wanted his wife with him in Washington, he knew she was much more at home in Boston. Her family and her volunteer work were there—as were her boys.

That's why he was torn when she asked Chance Demetrios to refer her to a specialist in D.C., claiming that she wanted to live there full-time with Jamison for the rest of the congressional session.

On one hand, he wanted her to be there with him. That's what he'd wanted since they'd reconciled; but on the other, he knew it wasn't realistic. In fact, it would be selfish to ask her to leave behind all the things she loved to be by his side. But in the end, she went back with him, returning to D.C. two days after their family dinner.

Exactly two weeks later, he could tell that Olivia was bored out of her mind. She'd tried to make friends, but the political circles in which they traveled were transient at best, and other times power-hungry and shallow. In a city of grand dames who were often traded in for trophy wives and mistresses who were vying to become trophy wives, a woman as beautiful as Olivia proved a substantial threat to those who were insecure in their station.

After wearing herself out shopping, setting up the kitchen in their Georgetown apartment so that she could cook, and going to see every ballet, museum exhibition and concert offered in the city, Olivia finally confessed to her husband that she missed

Boston. He was in the process of persuading her to go home for a visit when, out of the blue, his mother called him at the office to see when he and Olivia would be back in Boston because she wanted to have lunch with them.

This was a huge gesture on his mother's part. Though Jamison wanted to believe his words on Valentine's Day night had made an impact on her, she was Helen Mallory. Nobody told the Ice Queen how to behave.

So when Helen said, "I realize it's difficult for you to just pop back into town since you're not exactly next door. However, I'd like to get something on the calendar because… Well, Jamison, I simply feel as if Olivia and I need to bond," Jamison was determined to make it work.

"Mom, that sounds wonderful. I'm sure Olivia would be delighted to see you. The only problem is that I don't know when I can get away. You and Olivia should schedule something without me."

He leaned back in his leather chair, stretching his long legs out in front of him as he waited for his mother's reply. The pause seemed to last for years… nearly as long as the tense relations between his mother and his wife.

"I'd really hoped to see both of you together, Jamison. The luncheon date can wait until you're free."

"Mother, take Olivia to lunch and the three of us can schedule something for another time. This is important. Especially since she's carrying your grandchild."

Another stretch of silence loomed.

"Mother, call Olivia. Invite her to lunch."

Helen's sigh was audible even over the telephone line.

"All right. If you insist. I'll call her later this afternoon."

Jamison smiled to himself as he disconnected the call. All peace talks began with a single kind gesture. This was a huge step for his mother. One that made him very hopeful. One, he was certain, Olivia would appreciate.

Even so, he thought it might be a good idea to prepare her for his mother's call. He hit the speed dial key that connected him to Olivia's phone. As it rang, a warm glow of satisfaction coursed through him.

Fate was finally smiling on them.

After Olivia digested the idea of lunching with his mother, she'd see it that way, too.

Olivia hated hiding from Derek. To be completely truthful, that's what she'd been doing—hiding in Washington, D.C., from the implied threat he'd flung the last time she saw him.

At first, she brushed off the need to stay away as

simply wanting to be with her husband, but the wakeup call came—literally—after Helen phoned and invited her to come to Boston for a "girls' getaway" during which they'd go to a spa, take in a special production of *Swan Lake* staged by Olivia's former Harvard Ballet Company, and collaborate on a fundraiser for the Children's Home.

Olivia's first impulse had been *No!* because she couldn't imagine spending several awkward mani-pedi, salad-lunching days with her mother-in-law. Helen's call hadn't caught her off guard since Jamison had prepared her. Though she was only expecting a lunch date offer—not a "girls' getaway."

Though she was touched by Helen's effort to connect with her through a Children's Home fundraiser, Olivia wasn't kidding herself. Helen hadn't suddenly awakened a changed woman, wanting to embrace the daughter-in-law she'd kept at arm's length for years. Olivia understood that Helen's motivation was the baby Olivia was carrying. For a fleeting moment, she wondered what Helen would do if she knew the baby growing inside Olivia wasn't her biological child.

That's what made Olivia apprehensive. Because when she thought about coming home, she heard her brother's malevolent words about how they were due to talk about their "little secret," and the thought of coming face-to-face with her scheming, black-hearted brother was what had Olivia thinking about saying, "thanks, but no thanks," to Helen's generous offer.

While she was cautiously pleased by her mother-in-law's reaching out, the main thing that prevented her from completely burying her head, or even enticing Helen to come down to D.C. for their getaway, was what her avoiding Boston would cost the Children's Home. The support Helen Mallory could generate with a simple nod of approval was amazing. By attaching her name to a fundraiser, the potential was staggering.

So there was no way she could refuse.

There was no way Olivia could fly her down to Washington because that meant she wouldn't be able to give Helen a tour of the Children's Home—the final determining factor in exactly how much support Helen would offer, and Olivia was determined to get the maximum.

And if she followed Helen's rules, there was always the potential that she and her mother-in-law might actually bond. Wishful thinking, but a girl could dream. Olivia knew that nothing would make her husband happier than for Olivia and Helen to have a relationship. That in itself was enough incentive to keep believing.

She just had to figure out a way to keep her brother from ruining everything. Maybe the best defense was a little offense.

Maybe she needed to see her brother while she was there and set things straight once and for all. She had to stop hiding from Derek and go back to Boston. The reality was, if her brother wanted so badly to get this *message* to her, he could call her…or Jamison. He hadn't done so since they'd last spoken on Valentine's Day.

Derek was evil, but would he actually stoop so low as to blackmail his sister? She'd been over and over their conversation and she couldn't figure out what else he might have meant by it. Unless he was messing with her. But Derek didn't have the time or patience for games like that. Not unless he stood to gain from them.

Olivia was more than a little nervous when she met Helen at the Four Seasons Hotel in Boston. Of course, she was nervous about the one-on-one time with her mother-in-law, but she was also afraid of running into Derek.

He was the last person she wanted to see. Especially in the company of Helen.

She'd made up her mind to hope for the best. That's all she could do. It helped a little when

Jamison assured her that his mother was determined to make peace between them. Olivia could see how important it was to him. How could she not try?

It was simply two nights in a hotel suite; one day of spa treatments, which actually proved to be quite relaxing; and finally, on their second day together, the moment that Olivia had been waiting for—her chance to show off the Children's Home.

Though Helen had been a little aloof yesterday in the spa, Olivia reminded herself that just the fact that they were together—just the two of them, doing girly things together—was a milestone. Olivia knew not to expect Helen to make an effort at small talk. So she took the reins. By the time their limo stopped in front of the old Georgian mansion, Olivia had given Helen a rundown of the nonprofit's history and mission statement as well as their current financial needs.

"There are two small boys of whom I've become especially fond. I can't wait for you to meet them."

"Well, I certainly must say, you are quite passionate about this organization, aren't you?"

Olivia nodded. "Yes, I certainly am."

Wanting to give Helen the full experience, she led her up the wide steps to the front door, rather than escorting her around back to the kitchen entrance, where Olivia usually entered when she visited.

Pam was right there to greet them and welcome Helen. Since it was the middle of the day, Kevin was at school, but Danny was sitting in his usual spot with his beloved truck, spinning the wheels, every bit the same as the last time she saw him. It made her a little sad to think of him sitting there alone while his brother was in school. Had Pam talked to Danny's doctor about enrolling him in a program to help him?

She made a mental note to ask her before she left.

Pam led them on an extensive tour, which ended with her presenting Helen with a packet of information, including a sheet that prioritized the home's needs.

"As you can see, this is a worthy organization and we appreciate all the financial help we can get. Even though we're fiscally sound, we do encounter surprises periodically. For example, if you'll look over there, you'll see little Danny Kelso. He and his brother were orphaned on the evening after Christmas. It's a sad, sad story. No relatives. The parents hadn't made any provisions as to who was to get custody of the boys in the event of their death. Because of Danny's special needs, the Department of Children and Family asked us to take them in, even though technically we were at our budget-dictated capacity. We have a reserve fund that we can dip into for special cases such as this, so that we never have to turn away a child in need."

"Well, you can't keep them indefinitely. What will become of them?"

Pam glanced at Olivia and bit her bottom lip, a gesture that betrayed the fact that her friend had something on her mind.

"We're constantly working to place the children in loving families. In fact, just last week I successfully placed a ten-year-old girl. She'll be joining her adoptive family next week. As far as the Kelso boys are concerned, we're working hard to find a family to take them both, but because of Danny's autism, it's proving difficult."

Helen regarded Danny. "Autism, is it? I wondered what was wrong with him."

A mother tiger instinct that Olivia had never experienced before sprang to life inside her. The boy was autistic, but he wasn't deaf. Olivia had no idea if he knew when people were talking about him, but it didn't feel right carrying on as if he weren't in the room. Olivia had to bite her tongue to keep from telling Helen as much, but she held off. Embarrassing Helen Mallory was not the way to endear her to the Children's Home.

Pam's phone rang and she excused herself to answer it.

"I'm waiting for calls about the pending adoption and I see by the number this is one of them. If you'll excuse me, I have to take this."

Olivia took that opportunity to walk over to Danny. She knelt beside him. "Hi, honey. How are you?" Danny didn't look up. "I've missed you, little guy."

Still no response.

"I'm off to have another look around." Helen sounded bored and she left Olivia to her one-sided conversation with the boy.

Olivia missed her work at the Children's Home. She missed seeing the boys. She'd been checking on them often via phone calls to Pam, but it wasn't the same as being in the same room with them. The only thing missing now was Kevin. Olivia's heart ached with how much she wished she could see him.

A moment later, Pam reappeared. "I'm sorry about that—where did Helen go?"

"She's looking around."

"What do you think? Will she take on our cause?"

Frankly, Olivia had no idea. It had been impossible to read her mother-in-law's impassive poker face. Maybe it was a defense mechanism, because Helen had obviously perfected it a long time ago.

Pam glanced around the living room, as if she were making sure the coast was clear. "I have to tell you something. I'm not sure this is the best time to break it to you, but there's news."

Pam nodded in Danny's direction and Olivia's heart flip-flopped.

"You got him enrolled in the special education program?"

Pam grimaced. "Not exactly. Well, not *yet,* anyway." She gestured toward her office with a flick of her head. "Come in here where we can talk privately."

Every muscle in Olivia's body tensed. She had a feeling she knew what Pam was going to say before she said it. Even so, the words, *we've found a family that wants to adopt Danny,* sounded surreal when they bounced off her ears.

"What about Kevin?"

Pam shook her head. "I'm sorry. I'm afraid they can't take both of the boys. They want Danny. They're even willing to pay for private education for him."

Olivia felt as if her heart had been ripped out of her chest. She'd known it was going to be tough to get them into the same household, but it saddened her to think of those sweet boys spending the rest of their childhood in an orphanage. However, it was even sadder to think of them being split up and sent to different homes. Kevin would be devastated, too young to understand that this was a good opportunity for his little brother. She couldn't let him suffer another crushing blow like that.

What in the world was she going to do?

"Pam, please. No—"

But before Olivia could finish her sentence, Helen appeared in Pam's office doorway.

"I've seen enough. I'm ready to go. Thank you for your time, Ms. Wilson."

Pam looked at Olivia. Olivia looked at Helen.

Helen's face was impassive.

"What did you think? Will you help us with a fundraiser?" asked Olivia.

"I don't know yet. I'll have to get back to you. Come, Olivia, let's go."

Despite how much she wanted to stay, needed to stay, to ask Pam how they could rectify the situation and keep the boys together, Olivia tore herself away.

Neither woman said a word until they were tucked safely inside the limo. Olivia's head was too full of the news Pam had just sprung on her. Too full of sadness for Kevin. She barely heard her mother-in-law when she said, "Rule number one about supporting charities, Olivia, never commit yourself right out of the gate. Especially if you have every heartrending, poignant nonprofit in the northeast begging for your help. You can only choose a handful at best. And believe me, they're all worthy causes."

Helen sat and studied Olivia for a moment. Her perusal was so bold, it almost felt as if she were picking her apart piece by piece.

Olivia felt so weighted down, all she wanted to do

was turn away and rest her head on the car window. She had no fight in her right now and if Helen was going to pick her apart like a vulture on carrion, well—

"I mean, of course, I'm going to support your Children's Home, but we need not tell that Pam so right off the bat. Let her worry for a while. Oh, but that's right, you're on the board, aren't you?"

And then the strangest thing happened—Helen smiled. She actually smiled at Olivia.

"Congratulations, dear, I'm quite impressed with your charity. Together, you and I are going to raise a lot of money for it. But let's get you through this pregnancy first. Events of the magnitude that we're going to throw are exhausting." Helen reached out and laid a hand on Olivia's stomach. "I must confess, since you're going to be the mother of my grand-child, I realized that you and I needed some time to get to know each other better."

So Olivia had finally earned her spot next to Helen.

This was the equivalent of Helen patting the couch and beckoning Payton to sit next to her.

Olivia heard herself uttering words of thanks, but it was almost as if it were someone else saying the words. While she was glad the Children's Home would benefit, she was heartsick over the news that the Kelso boys would be split up. And underneath it all, she couldn't help but feel like a fraud.

What would Helen do if she knew the baby Olivia was carrying wasn't really hers? It was Jamison's seed fertilizing some mystery woman's egg. Olivia was just the incubator.

Well, Helen would never find out.

Chapter Thirteen

Olivia was relieved when her visit to Boston passed with no contact from Derek. Actually, it put her worried mind to rest.

Had she misunderstood what he'd said?

Maybe.

Who knew?

But he had been pretty cryptic that night in the kitchen. Why?

Forget *why*. She really didn't want to know.

Still, that didn't keep her from pondering the puzzle and worrying over the pending adoption of Danny Kelso. She told Jamison, hoping that somehow, someway they could find a solution that would allow the boys to stay together. It might be possible because the adoption process was not going smoothly. Pam had even decided to wait until all the paperwork had been approved before breaking the news to Kevin.

With this scant glimmer of hope, Olivia prayed for a miracle that somehow, someway her boys could stay together.

It was a much-needed distraction when the invitation for the State dinner honoring the president of Tunisia and his wife arrived in the mail.

Jamison had been so busy with work, and they'd both been so tired most evenings, that they hadn't gone out as a couple in a while.

It was fun shopping for her dress and planning for their big night out. It was especially exciting when she discovered that she'd gained a dress size.

At this point she wasn't really *showing* as much as she was starting to fill out. Her breasts were fuller—which Jamison loved—and she was starting to lose the definition in her waist.

Since the new silver-beaded gown she bought for the dinner was only one size larger than what she normally wore, she'd easily be able to take it in after she was back to her pre-pregnancy weight.

With all the shopping and preparation of getting

ready for the important dinner, Olivia wasn't surprised that she was exhausted the day of the event.

After she got back from having her hair done, she lay down and rested for a couple of hours, but even that didn't help refresh her.

When it was time to get ready, she was actually feeling a little bit nauseated, but she thought it was just because she was hungry. As she was getting ready, she ate some toast and drank a cup of herbal tea.

That seemed to take the edge off of it, and she was glad, because the event tonight was so important to Jamison.

Influential people would be there. Those whose support it would be necessary to secure if he was to gain the nomination for the 2016 presidential race.

That seemed like lifetimes away. In fact, by then, their baby would be seven years old and would probably have a sibling—just the thought of that gave Olivia a boost of energy.

But as far as the presidential race was concerned, the clock was ticking. Jamison needed to utilize every opportunity that came his way and, as the future first lady, Olivia needed to be by his side.

Especially tonight.

So she donned her silver gown and white gloves. She helped Jamison fix his bow tie, and together they set out to win over the decision makers.

When they arrived at the White House's north portico, the place was alive with honor guards from all branches of the military in full dress uniform. A few minutes later, Jamison and Olivia looked on as the President and First Lady formally greeted the president of Tunisia and his wife.

They were among a scant handful invited to join the pre-dinner cocktail party. As they joined the dignitaries, they paused at the top of the grand staircase to give the media an opportunity to shoot photos before disappearing upstairs for cocktails.

That's when Olivia first started to feel the cramping. At first she wasn't sure. She brushed it off as exhaustion and promised herself that she'd sleep all day tomorrow if her body needed it.

Jamison was in top form tonight and she couldn't hold him back. Especially when the President himself introduced Jamison as "a man to watch."

As they spoke, Olivia greeted the Tunisian first lady and exchanged pleasantries. But she was relieved when the woman was whisked off to meet the next person, because Olivia had to sit down. The cramping was getting worse.

No. This can't be happening. Not tonight. Not any night.

She managed to hold herself together until the entourage descended the grand staircase and

paused in the entrance hall to listen to the Marine
Corps Band play "Hail to the Chief" and the
Tunisian anthem.

Finally, after the other formal festivities, they
walked down the Cross Hall to the state dining room,
full of tables lavishly set with gold-edged official
china that sat atop gold-and-white tablecloths vying
for space with riots of white-flowered centerpieces
and glowing candelabras.

Olivia knew she was in trouble and had to leave
the dining room before the President took the lectern
to deliver his speech. She excused herself to the
ladies' room.

She leaned in to Jamison and whispered, "I'll be
right back."

Jamison asked, "Are you all right?"

"I'm fine." She smiled through a cramp. "I just
need to use the ladies' room before the President
starts his address."

Jamison and the other men at the table stood as
she rose from her seat. She felt a bit light-headed
as she traversed the room to the door, where a staff
member opened it for her and discreetly directed her
to the lavatory.

As soon as she was inside, she felt a sticky
dampness between her legs and thought she might
fall apart. But she couldn't. She had to stay calm. She

had to think logically. She took her BlackBerry from her purse and dialed her doctor's number.

Unfortunately, it went directly to the answering service, where she left an urgent message. She knew she had to get off her feet. With the help of staff she found in Cross Hall, she was able to find her driver, who immediately took her home.

She called Jamison from the limo, but as she expected, the call went to voice mail because he'd silenced his phone.

She purposely steadied her voice and left him a message. "Jamison, it's me. I don't want you to worry, but I wasn't feeling well and I went home to lie down. Please don't worry or rush. I'll be fine."

When Olivia didn't return after fifteen minutes, Jamison excused himself and went to look for her. Out in the hall he paused to check his phone and saw the message.

The moment he heard her voice, he knew she wasn't fine and felt an urgency to be with her. By the time he was ready to go, the driver had returned and confirmed that he had just dropped Mrs. Mallory off at their Georgetown residence.

It momentarily staved off Jamison's worries when the driver told him that she'd appeared tired and was quiet, but nothing alarming had happened on the ride home.

Everything changed when Jamison entered the apartment and found Olivia collapsed on the bathroom floor.

Not only did she lose the baby, but she'd injured herself when she fainted and hit her head on the tile floor.

The attending physician seemed to take pleasure in telling her that she was lucky that she hadn't ended up with a cerebral hematoma, which could have cost her her life.

But Olivia didn't seem to care. All she wanted to do was sleep, because when she was awake all she did was cry over the child they'd lost.

Jamison felt utterly helpless—nothing he tried seemed to help his wife.

Finally, he excused himself to call her family. He had to let them know that Olivia was in the hospital...and that she'd miscarried.

Strangely enough, the only person he was able to reach was Derek.

"Derek, it's Jamison. I'm afraid I have some bad news."

After he'd relayed the news to his brother-in-law,

and established that she was, indeed, going to be all right, he was taken aback when Derek lit into him.

"Are you finally going to ease up on pressuring her to give you a child?"

Tired from having spent a sleepless night at Olivia's bedside, Jamison flinched at Derek's tone.

"Excuse me? What are you talking about?"

"This is your fault, man. You and your overbearing mother. Olivia only underwent those treatments to please you and your demanding family. If anything happens to her, your ass is history."

His harsh words bounced off Jamison's ears like crashing cymbals. He'd never pressured Olivia. In fact, he'd been the reluctant one. But he certainly wasn't going to stand there and argue with Derek when Olivia was lying in a hospital bed.

Still, he couldn't let it go without putting in his two cents. "I don't know where you get off saying that. Olivia wanted a child just as badly as I did, but I'm certainly not obligated to explain anything to you. I just called to let you know that your sister is in the hospital and to ask if you could pass along the message since I've already tried the others and couldn't reach them."

"She confided in me. Told me what a jackass you've been. That your marriage was on the rocks. That's where I get off saying these things. You have no idea the lengths my sister has gone to to please you. You've got to stop pushing her to get pregnant or you're going to kill her."

With that, Derek hung up the phone, leaving Jamison's head spinning as he tried to figure out exactly what had just happened.

Olivia had confided in Derek?

He and Derek had never seen eye-to-eye. There was something about the guy that always seemed a little off—unlike Paul, who was the best brother-in-law a guy could ask for.

He couldn't believe that Olivia would open up to Derek of all people. But obviously she had.

You have no idea the lengths my sister has gone to to please you.

Was he talking about the trial separation? The fertility treatments?

Jamison had hated what she'd gone through. The only reason he'd supported it again this time was because she so desperately wanted a baby.

But it was becoming clear that wasn't going to happen. He couldn't stand by while she continued to put her body through such turmoil. Because it was obvious that she wasn't strong enough and each miscarriage seemed to be more severe.

He didn't like Derek very much, but he did agree with him on one point: enough was enough.

* * *

Two days later, the doctor released Olivia, who was restricted to limited activity. She tried to convince Jamison that she was fine. Still, he insisted on taking the rest of the week off and staying home with her.

There really wasn't anything for him to do other than pick up takeout food and take out the trash, but Olivia couldn't convince him to return to work.

"I'm sure I'm up to throwing away a cardboard carton, Jamison," she said. But he wouldn't hear of it. It seemed as if he simply wanted to be near her. Sometimes she'd look up from the book she was reading or glance over at him while they were watching TV and catch him staring at her.

"What's the matter?" she'd ask.

He'd shake his head and blink as if he were clearing cobwebs from his mind.

Of course, the only thing on Olivia's mind was talking to Chance Demetrios about how long she needed to wait before they could try another in vitro procedure.

The following Sunday, as they sat enjoying bagels and the Sunday paper, she said, "I'm flying back to Boston on Tuesday. I have an appointment with Dr. Demetrios. We're going to discuss when I can start the process again."

Jamison put the paper down and looked at her as

if she was crazy. "Olivia. Please. You can't go through this again."

"Yes, I can."

"Well, *I* can't," he insisted. "Look, I talked to Derek while you were in the hospital."

Derek? Olivia's body went numb with shock. "And what did he say?"

Jamison simply looked at her for a minute and, though she didn't think it possible, the longer he stared, the more frightened she got.

"He told me…" Jamison stopped mid-sentence and shook his head.

Oh, my God.

"He told you what?" she demanded.

He shook his head again. "Let's just not do this again, okay?"

"Jamison, I'm sorry. I wanted to tell you, but I didn't know how you'd take it."

Her husband's face clouded with confusion. "Tell me what?"

Uh-oh. Maybe she'd spoken too soon.

He knew that look. She was keeping something from him. Probably the same thing that Derek was hinting at when he told Jamison he had no idea of *the lengths my sister has gone to to please you.*

"What did Derek tell you?" she insisted.

He knew it wasn't fair, but his instincts were telling him that perhaps his wife hadn't been putting all her cards on the table. So he opted for an old bluff he'd employed when he used to practice law.

"He told me everything."

First, Olivia's face turned white. Then it crumpled. As much as he hated to see his wife in mental pain, especially after what she'd been through physically, he needed to know the whole story.

"How could he do that to me?" Olivia's voice was a shock-induced hoarse whisper.

Every muscle in Jamison's body tensed. "Why don't you start from the beginning and tell me your version of the story?"

And she did. Telling him again about the appointment with Chance Demetrios where she learned that she was not able to have any more children and then about how she'd cried on Derek's shoulder and he'd come up with the plan to switch the eggs.

Jamison's blood started to simmer, and with each detail of how she'd deceived him, how she'd taken matters into her own hands and purposely left him out of the decision-making process about *his* child, his blood began to boil until it finally reached the point where he knew he had to get away from her to process all the lies and deception. Because sitting here, looking at her sad eyes and beautiful face, he was tempted to overlook the fact that she'd lied to him about something so serious.

And in a big way.

Lies and deception. Not exactly the same brand that wrecked his parents' marriage, but stripped down to the bones, a lie was a lie was a lie.

He'd had to trick her into telling him the truth. He didn't know if he could live with a woman he couldn't trust.

He certainly couldn't live a life marred by lies and deception.

He stood.

"Where are you going?" Her voice was panicked.

"I need to go out for a while. I need time to think, time to process things. I need to figure out how you could lie to me about something so important."

She reached out to him.

"Jamison, please don't go. We need to talk this out."

He shook his head and let himself out the front door.

Chapter Fourteen

They decided it would be best if Olivia moved back to Boston while Jamison finished the congressional session. Olivia didn't like it, but he said he needed time to sort things out and she wanted to give him room.

She let him know that she loved him and would be waiting for him…forever, if that's how long it took.

Back in Boston, as she put her things away, she realized that they were back to square one. No, this time it felt like square minus one, and she didn't know if the damage could be fixed.

It was Derek's fault.

She wasn't blaming him for offering her the donor egg or for encouraging her to deceive her husband. She took full responsibility for that. She should've told Jamison.

That way, Derek wouldn't have had anything to use against her. How could he have done it? How could he have gone straight to Jamison and spilled the beans without first giving her the chance to clean up her own mess and tell her husband herself?

First the blackmail innuendos, now this.

As far as she was concerned, her relationship with her brother was over.

But first she intended to give him a piece of her mind.

Olivia drove to the institute and went immediately to Derek's office. She pushed open the closed door and found him talking on the phone.

"Get off the phone, Derek," she said, like a woman possessed. Suddenly, she knew how Danny Kelso must feel when he threw back his head and wailed at the top of his lungs. That's what she wanted to do now.

But since she still possessed a modicum of self-control, she refrained.

She did, however, raise her voice a few decibels when Derek ignored her and kept talking.

"I said get off the phone, Derek. I need to talk to you now!"

This time she got his attention. He ended the conversation.

"What the hell is wrong with you? Can't you see I was on a business call?"

"Yes, I could see that. I just decided to come in here and start messing up your life like you've messed up mine. Oh, but there's one problem—you don't have a life. Is that why you derive such pleasure in messing with other people's?"

He threw his hands up in the air. "Olivia. What are you talking about?"

She wanted to take her hand and swipe it across his desk, knock everything on it to the floor. She wanted to grab him by the shirtsleeves and shake him until his teeth rattled.

"You know what I'm talking about. You know what you told Jamison."

Either he was a good actor or he truly was puzzled. "I talked to Jamison, but I didn't really tell him anything. Except that I thought he needed to call off the dogs when it came to pressuring you into pumping out babies."

"You told him about the donor egg."

"No I did not."

"But he knew."

"Well, he didn't hear it from me."

Derek shrugged, to indicate case dismissed. Brother off the hook.

"There's nobody else he could've heard it from, if not you. What I don't understand is why you would set up your own sister for extortion, Derek. That's about as low as it gets."

His eyes shuttered.

"I have no idea what you're talking about."

A different look from the adamant way he'd denied telling Jamison passed over his face. A completely different demeanor. Suddenly Olivia wanted to back-pedal, because she was sure she'd missed something.

"You know what I'm talking about. The Valentine's Day dinner party at my house when Jamison and I told the family I was pregnant. You followed me into the kitchen and said that we needed to *talk*. What did you want to talk about, Derek? A payment plan so that you'd keep my secret?"

It turned her stomach, but she could tell that's what he'd been setting her up for. That he hadn't contacted her…well, maybe he'd still felt a murmur of a heart or a conscience or a soul and he'd chickened out.

"I just don't understand why you'd feel compelled to tell my husband what you did while I was lying in a hospital bed not even twenty-four hours after my miscarriage? What was in it for you? Could you just not stand to see somebody happy?"

He glanced down at his hands, fisted them, and then flexed them before he answered.

"I didn't intend to blackmail you. What I wanted to talk to you about was the blood type of the donor. After the fact, I realized that your blood types didn't match and that could've caused a snag in your seamless plan."

Olivia studied her brother, trying to determine whether he was telling the truth or not. She wanted to believe him, but she couldn't.

"Show me proof, Derek. Call up the file of this donor and show me what type of blood she has."

He scratched his nose. "I can't. I destroyed the original file."

"You destroyed the file? You expect me to believe that?"

He blinked rapidly. "I couldn't just transfer her eggs to you and leave the file empty. That's called a paper trail. Someone could've followed it."

She wasn't buying it.

"You'd go to great pains to destroy a file to make the scheme, as you called it, seamless. Yet you'd forget all about the red flag of blood type. Doesn't make sense. This is your business. It seems like blood types would be right up there in standard info right next to dark hair and dark eyes."

His mouth flattened into a hard, straight line. "My

background is in business, Livie, not medicine. I had no idea what to look for beyond skin, hair and eye color. I was trying to make sure the baby looked like you. It didn't occur to me to match the donor's blood type with yours until was deleting the original file and saw it."

He scratched his nose again. She'd read that was often a signal that someone was lying. But who knew for sure? Especially with Derek.

"I guess I'll really never know the truth, will I?" Derek shrugged.

"I many not have solid proof that it really was the blood I was concerned with, but I do have proof that I wasn't the one who told your husband about the donor eggs. If you don't believe me, just ask him."

She left the institute more confused than when she arrived. Strange how her heart wanted to believe that he might be telling the truth, but her head still wasn't buying his story.

She got home and the place seemed so empty. The Valentine's Day dinner, the girl's getaway with Helen and all those nights that she and Jamison had made love until the sun came up seemed like a distant memory.

She sat in her bedroom window seat, gazing out over the Gardens, which were just starting to show the first signs of spring, and held the phone for a long time before she could bring herself to make the call.

When she finally did, she was surprised when he answered on the first ring.

"Hi, it's me. I'm sorry. I'm *so* sorry. I never intended to lie to you. It just seemed like my last chance. Our last chance. And I so desperately wanted to give you a child. Can you ever forgive me?"

As much as Jamison disliked Derek, he had to give the guy credit. Derek might possibly have saved his and Olivia's marriage.

Despite how rough around the edges and unpalatable the guy could be, he was right. Jamison and his family were partially to blame for Olivia's desperation to have a child.

A desperation that drove her to go so far she'd do something that forced her to lie to him.

Maybe it was because she'd never lied before. Or maybe it was because Jamison felt partially responsible. It was definitely because he still loved her, despite what had happened and maybe even because of the lengths she'd gone to for him. But two days after they'd talked, he'd hopped on a Boston-bound plane and found himself wandering through the Public Garden at noon.

Pam had told him he'd find her there. Olivia had taken the Kelso boys on a picnic.

As he rounded a copse of trees that shaded a statue, there she sat on a red plaid picnic blanket with Danny in her lap. The boy held his truck, spinning the wheels, seeming perfectly content sitting there.

She was saying something to Kevin, who was running around the grass in front of the blanket throwing a football up in the air.

But her mouth froze mid-sentence when she saw Jamison. For a moment, he couldn't speak, either. Seeing her sitting there with the boys was a picture.

They looked like a family. The small, dark-haired boys could've easily passed for her children. Not much of him and his Celtic coloring, but then again, anyone knew that dark hair and eyes were usually the dominant gene.

He stood there savoring the picture for a moment as everything important snapped into perfect focus. Suddenly the world seemed to make sense, or at least it seemed as if it could if the four of them became a family.

Then Olivia finally found her voice and said, "I'm so glad you're here. I thought I'd lost you forever."

He shook his head and lowered himself onto the blanket. "What kind of fool would I be if I let you walk out of my life? I'm not saying it was okay to keep those things from me—there is nothing you can't come to me with. But I love you and I'm glad you're my wife."

He leaned in and kissed her tenderly on the lips.

"Truck!"

When he looked up, Danny was offering him the toy truck and Kevin was asking him to toss the football.

As he was throwing the ball with the older boy, he glanced at the love of his life sitting on the blanket like the Madonna with her child. He knew exactly what she was thinking because he was thinking the same thing.

There had been snags in Danny's adoption. He had to believe that had happened because the boys were meant to be their children. Part of their family.

The family they chose.

* * * * *

*Look for the next installment
in the new Special Edition continuity,*
THE BABY CHASE

Sara Beth O'Connell's boss asks her to spy on
scientist Ted Bonner—and the more time the
nurse spends with the sexy doctor, the faster
they move from business to pleasure. But will a
secret in Sara's past threaten their budding
romance?

Don't miss
THE DOCTOR'S PREGNANT BRIDE?
by Susan Crosby
On sale March 2010,
wherever Silhouette Books are sold.

*Rancher Ramsey Westmoreland's temporary cook
is way too attractive for his liking.
Little does he know Chloe Burton came to his
ranch with another agenda entirely....*

That man across the street had to be, without a doubt, the most handsome man she'd ever seen.

Chloe Burton's pulse beat rhythmically as he stopped to talk to another man in front of a feed store. He was tall, dark and every inch of sexy—from his Stetson to the well-worn leather boots on his feet. And from the way his jeans and Western shirt fit his broad muscular shoulders, it was quite obvious he had everything it took to separate the men from the boys. The combination was enough to corrupt any woman's mind and had her weakening even from a distance. Her body felt flushed. It was hot. Unsettled.

Over the past year the only male who had gotten her time and attention had been the e-mail. That was simply pathetic, especially since now she was practically drooling simply at the sight of a man. Even his stance—both hands in his jeans pockets, legs braced apart, was a pose she would carry to her dreams.

And he was smiling, evidently enjoying the conversation being exchanged. He had dimples, incredibly sexy dimples in not one but both cheeks.

"What are you staring at, Clo?"

Chloe nearly jumped. She'd forgotten she had a lunch date. She glanced over the table at her best friend from college, Lucia Conyers.

"Take a look at that man across the street in the blue shirt, Lucia. Will he not be perfect for Denver's first issue of *Simply Irresistible* or what?" Chloe asked with so much excitement she almost couldn't stand it.

She was the owner of *Simply Irresistible*, a magazine for today's up-and-coming woman. Their once-a-year Irresistible Man cover, which highlighted a man the magazine felt deserved the honor, had increased sales enough for Chloe to open a Denver office.

When Lucia didn't say anything but kept staring, Chloe's smile widened. "Well?"

Lucia glanced across the booth at her. "Since you asked, I'll tell you what I see. One of the Westmorelands—Ramsey Westmoreland. And yes, he'd be perfect for the cover, but he won't do it."

Chloe raised a brow. "He'd get paid for his services, of course."

Lucia laughed and shook her head. "Getting paid won't be the issue, Clo—Ramsey is one of the wealthiest sheep ranchers in this part of Colorado.

But everyone knows what a private person he is. Trust me—he won't do it."

Chloe couldn't help but smile. The man was the epitome of what she was looking for in a magazine cover and she was determined that whatever it took, he would be it.

"Umm, I don't like that look on your face, Chloe. I've seen it before and know exactly what it means."

She watched as Ramsey Westmoreland entered the store with a swagger that made her almost breathless. She *would* be seeing him again.

Look for Silhouette Desire's
HOT WESTMORELAND NIGHTS
by Brenda Jackson,
available March 9 wherever books are sold.

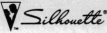

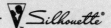

SPECIAL EDITION

FROM *USA TODAY* BESTSELLING AUTHOR
CHRISTINE RIMMER

A BRIDE FOR JERICHO BRAVO

Marnie Jones had long ago buried her wild-child
impulses and opted to be "safe," romantically
speaking. But one look at born rebel Jericho Bravo
and she began to wonder if her thrill-seeking side
was about to be revived. Because if ever there was
a man worth taking a chance on, there he was,
right within her grasp....

*Available in March
wherever books are sold.*

Visit Silhouette Books at www.eHarlequin.com

SSE65511

*Two families torn apart by secrets and desire
are about to be reunited in*

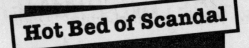

a sexy new duet by

Kelly Hunter

EXPOSED: MISBEHAVING WITH THE MAGNATE

#2905 Available March 2010

Gabriella Alexander returns to the French vineyard she
was banished from after being caught in flagrante with the
owner's son Lucien Duvalier—only to finish what they started!

REVEALED: A PRINCE AND A PREGNANCY

#2913 Available April 2010

Simone Duvalier wants Rafael Alexander and always has, but
they both get more than they bargained for when a night of
passion and a royal revelation rock their world!

HARLEQUIN
Ambassadors

*Want to share your passion
for reading Harlequin® Books?*

Become a Harlequin Ambassador!

Harlequin Ambassadors are a group
of passionate and well-connected readers
who are willing to share their joy of reading
Harlequin® books with family and friends.

You'll be sent all the tools you need to spark
great conversation, including free books!

All we ask is that you share the romance
with your friends and family!

You'll also be invited to have a say in
new book ideas and exchange opinions
with women just like you!

**To see if you qualify* to be
a Harlequin Ambassador, please visit
www.HarlequinAmbassadors.com.**

*Please note that not everyone who applies to be a Harlequin Ambassador will
qualify. For more information please visit www.HarlequinAmbassadors.com.

Thank you for your participation.

BAP09BPA

REQUEST YOUR FREE BOOKS!
2 FREE NOVELS PLUS 2 FREE GIFTS!

SPECIAL EDITION
Life, Love and Family!

Devastating, dark-hearted and...
looking for brides.

Look for

BOUGHT:
DESTITUTE YET DEFIANT
by *Sarah Morgan*
#2902

From the lowliest slums to Millionaire's Row...
these men have everything now but their brides—
and they'll settle for nothing less than the best!

Available March 2010
from Harlequin Presents!